Bitterbrush

Angela K. Black

ABCDE Publishing

Published by:

ABCDE Publishing
P.O. Box 374
Spanish Fork, Utah 84660-0374
(801) 798-8832

Edited by Jody Reid

Cover art by Becky Oldham

Library of Congress Catalog Card Number: 94-72417

ISBN: 0-9642571-0-6

Printed in the United States of America

I would like to express my deepest gratitude to my reading committee: Cheryl Dudley, Kass Black, Camille Larsen, Robyn Brock and Marcella Nichols.

A huge "thank you" to my editor, Jody Reid. You're the absolute best! And to Becky Oldham for using her remarkable talents in creating my cover.

My love, thanks and sincere appreciation go to my parents for their unending love and support; to Cheryl for her encouragement, support and unbelievable patience; to Don Roylance, for keeping me "on-line"; to Fritz, for being the best friend a sister ever had; to my family, friends (the greatest teammates in the world!) and all of you who believed in me. Watch out, I'm just warming up!

*This book is lovingly dedicated
to my parents,
George and Kass Black.*

Bitterbrush

CHAPTER 1

"This one's for you, Hal!" the tall, broad man bellowed as he hung up the phone.

Harold Lund looked up at his captain and smiled halfheartedly. He picked up the receiver and pushed the flashing red button. "Sergeant Lund."

"I would like to report a missing person." The woman's voice was faint and shaky.

"And your name is?" Hal fished a cigarette from a freshly opened pack. There was silence on the other end. "Ma'am?"

"Yes, I'm here."

"I'll need your name for the report." Hal put the cigarette in his mouth and searched his pockets for a lighter.

The caller cleared her throat. "Helen Connor."

Lund rummaged quickly through his desk drawers. He took the cigarette from his mouth and hurled it to the desk. Picking up his pen, he returned his attention to the caller. "And who is it that's missing?"

"My daughter, Elizabeth Harrison."

"How old is your daughter, Mrs. Connor?"

The caller paused. "Twenty-five. Wait—twenty-six."

"Okay . . ."

"Yes, twenty-six."

"How long has she been missing?"

"I'm not really sure."

"Okay." Lund's irritation was nearing a peak. "When did it first occur to you that she might be missing?"

"Well, three days ago she asked me to take Ryan for a day or two while she went out of town."

"Ryan?" Hal interjected.

"Ryan's my grandson, her son."

"Okay, go ahead." Hal took notes as their conversation continued.

"She told me she was going to Park City to get away from Craig and that she would be in touch with me, but I haven't heard from her. She was scheduled . . ."

Hal interrupted the woman, "Who is Craig?"

"Her husband. They're going through a divorce." There was silence on the phone as Hal jotted notes on a sheet of paper. She continued, "Liz wouldn't do this. Something's got to be wrong. She's never been away from Ryan without calling. It's just not like her."

"Did she tell you where she'd be staying?"

"No, she didn't say, but I've called all the hotels looking for her, and she's not registered at any of them. Her work called this morning—she didn't show up for her shift yesterday."

Hal was struggling to turn his attention away from his craving for nicotine and toward Elizabeth Harrison. "Mrs. Connor, would it be all right if I came out to your home to ask a few questions?"

"Yes, of course."

Lund scribbled her address on the bottom corner of the paper and hung up the phone. He grabbed the open pack of cigarettes from his desk and shoved them into the pocket of his brown sports jacket.

"Jim, I've got a missing person here." Lund waved a blank report form over his head as he walked toward a bulky man who sat huddled over his desk. The man mumbled an indiscernible reply and wedged his excessive frame free from his chair.

"Who's driving, Hal?" Jim Webber asked as the two men walked through the station doors that led to the parking garage.

"I'll drive." Lund retrieved a cigarette from his pocket as they neared their gray Corsica. "You got a light?" He looked up at Jim.

"Now, why would I have a light?" Jim walked over to the passenger side of the car and waited for Hal to get in and unlock his door.

Lund started the car as his partner got in. He pushed the cigarette lighter in, then handed Mrs. Connor's address to Jim.

"So, what's the story?" Jim asked.

Hal Lund put the glowing red end of the lighter to the cigarette that hung from his lips and sucked until warm smoke filled his lungs. He replaced the lighter and began backing out. "Twenty-six-year-old woman going through a divorce took off to Park City for a couple of days and left her kid with her mother." He took another drag from his cigarette. "The mother hasn't heard from her, and she's getting nervous."

"Probably at one of the resorts up there with her husband's best friend!" Jim took a Hershey's Chocolate Kiss from his jacket pocket and popped it in his mouth.

*   *   *

"Nice house!" Jim tossed another silver wrapper to the floor of the sedan as they pulled into the driveway at 2487 Heather Road. Hal grabbed a leather-bound notebook as he exited the car. "My ex-wife's house is almost this big," Jim said with bitterness as the two men neared the front door.

"Mrs. Connor?" Lund reached for a pen in his jacket pocket.

"Yes."

"I'm Sergeant Lund. I spoke with you on the phone. This is Officer Webber."

"Come in." The silver-haired woman turned and led them to a spacious room with vaulted ceilings. The carpet and draperies were white, the furniture pale blue. It was spotless, almost having an antiseptic air about it. "Please, make yourselves comfortable. I appreciate you coming."

Hal and Jim took a seat on the long sofa that faced a matching colonial chair.

"Can I get you anything?" Helen smiled.

"No, ma'am," Jim stated. "Mrs. Connor, we just need to get more details, so we can help you find your daughter."

"Gramma!" A little, dark-haired boy came running into the room. "Gramma, can I have . . ." The boy stopped in his tracks as his big brown eyes fell upon the men perched on the couch.

"This is my grandson, Ryan." Helen walked over to the boy and bent down. "What is it, honey?"

Ryan stood silently staring at Hal and Jim for a moment, and then in a quiet voice he spoke, "Gramma, can I have another cookie?" He made the request of Helen without taking his eyes off the police officers.

Helen tousled the boy's hair. "Sure, honey, but don't make a mess." With that, the boy was gone as quickly as he had come.

"I've watched Ryan for Liz before," Helen walked over to the empty chair and sat down with a sigh, "but she usually calls to talk to him, you know, make sure everything is all right. I haven't heard from her since Tuesday—that's when she left. Feldman's called here this morning. Apparently, she was supposed to be back to work yesterday, and she hasn't called them, either."

"She works at Feldman's Department Store?" Hal glanced up from his notepad.

"Yes, part-time. She's a salesclerk there." Helen ran her finger back and forth across the smooth wooden arm of her chair.

"Which Feldman's?"

"The one in Fashion Place Mall," Helen replied.

"Does she live with her husband?" Jim piped in.

"No, they're separated. He moved into an apartment in August."

"What's her address, ma'am?"

"Seventeen forty-six Lakecrest."

"You said you've tried to reach her?" Hal reached into his pocket and felt for his cigarettes. Thinking better of it, he left them there.

"I've called all the hotels, and if she's in one of them, she's not using her name." Helen shifted in her seat and smoothed her slacks.

Jim leaned forward. "Have you spoken to her husband?"

"I tried calling last night, but I just got his answering machine."

"You said on the phone that your daughter wanted to get away from her husband." Hal looked at Helen. "What exactly did she say?"

"Well, Craig—her husband—apparently scared her when they were arguing Monday night."

"Did she say that?" Hal asked.

"Yes. She told me that things have gotten pretty tense between the two of them the past couple of weeks. She said she was afraid of him."

"Do you have a picture of your daughter?" Jim lightly drummed his fingers on the coffee table.

"Yes." Helen rose from her chair. "I'll be right back."

Helen walked out of the room and Jim looked at his partner. "Do you think it's anything?" he asked.

"I think the divorce is probably getting to her, so she needed some space. I'll bet we have it wrapped up before we go home tonight." Hal smiled with confidence.

Helen walked back into the room with a few photos in her hand. "This was taken at Ryan's fourth birthday party in February." She handed Hal a photo of a smiling, light-haired woman holding the boy they had seen earlier on her lap. "And this was taken at her wedding." The second photo was of the same woman, standing next to a dark, handsome young man.

"May we take them?" Hal gestured at the photos.

"Of course."

Hal handed the photos to Jim. "Does she have a car?"

"Yes. It's a little white one. A Toyota, I think."

"Do you know what year it is?"

"Oh, I don't know. It's two, maybe three years old."

"Do you know the license plate number?" Hal continued with his questions.

"No. No, I don't. I'm sorry."

"That's okay." Hal stood and took a card from his shirt pocket. "Call us if you hear from her. We'll check this out and be in touch with you." He picked his notepad up from the coffee table, placed the photos inside, and nodded to his partner.

Helen followed them to the door. "If there's anything else you need from me, please call."

"We sure will, Mrs. Connor." Jim smiled at Helen and then turned to join Hal on the porch. The two walked to their car in silence.

Hal lit a cigarette from the car lighter and pulled out of the driveway. He turned to Jim. "Where's Lakecrest?"

"Sugarhouse."

Hal followed Jim's directions to 1746 Lakecrest Drive. It was a small, one-level home that sat on the corner of a tree-lined street. It was obviously an older home that had recently been renovated. The front door faced east, offering a beautiful view of the Wasatch Mountains. Jim and Hal walked up the steps to the large wooden deck that served as a porch. Jim stepped up to the door and knocked several times. The morning's *Salt Lake Tribune* and ones from the previous two days lay at Hal's feet. He looked up at the mailbox, brimming with letters. A small gold plate on the box read "The Harrisons." Jim knocked again and the two men waited another moment.

Jim put his hands up to the small pane of glass on the front door and tried to see in, but to no avail.

"I'm going to walk around to the back door." Hal stepped off the porch and walked through the autumn leaves that covered the Harrison's lawn to the south side of the house. A tall redwood fence started at the garage and surrounded the backyard. Hal tried peering over it, but his six-foot frame was several inches too short. He knocked loudly at the door, but again there was no answer.

Jim walked around from the front of the house. "I don't think anyone's in there. Where do you want to take it from here?"

Hal thought for a moment before answering. "Let's head down to the mall. I'll talk with her supervisor while you try to get hold of her husband."

*   *   *

Hal sat in a metal frame chair in the business office on Feldman's third floor. He rubbed his fingers across his chin and began planning the weekend in his mind. Steve was putting tile down in the bathroom of his new house, and Hal had offered his help. Hal always looked forward to spending time with his oldest son. Steve was probably Hal's best friend now, the only person he felt he could really talk to.

"Detective?" A middle-aged woman with short blonde hair approached Hal.

Hal stood and offered his hand in greeting. "Yes."

"Hi. I'm Sarah Hepworth, Liz's supervisor." Her look was one of concern.

"Ms. Hepworth, I'm Harold Lund, with the Salt Lake Police Department. We're trying to locate Mrs. Harrison and understand she was scheduled to work yesterday. Have you heard from her?" Hal opened his notebook and poised his pencil on the page ready to write.

"Liz was scheduled to work eleven to four yesterday and nine to three today. She's never missed a shift before, not without calling in."

"Did she mention anything about leaving town to you or any of her coworkers?" Hal glanced up from his notebook.

"No, she didn't say anything to me Tuesday. I don't know if she said anything to anyone else."

"So, she was at work Tuesday?"

"Yes. She worked until four. She was off Wednesday. She has every Wednesday off," Sarah answered, smiling politely.

"Did she seem upset or preoccupied Tuesday?"

"I didn't talk to her much, but she seemed fine. She didn't seem any different than usual. Liz has always been kind of private. She's very nice, gets along well with everybody, but she's never been one to talk at length about her personal life." Sarah watched Hal as he took notes, then added an afterthought. "She's an excellent worker."

"Do you know who would have been the last one to see her here Tuesday?"

"I can look at the schedule and see who might have left the same time she did. I could also ask around to see if someone saw her leave or talked with her."

"That would be great." Hal watched as the woman disappeared behind a wooden door marked "Personnel." He sat back down and looked over the notes he had taken so far. He was anxious to hear whether Jim had been successful at tracking down Craig Harrison. Hal looked up as the door opened again.

"Mr. Lund, these are the names and phone numbers of people who worked with Liz that day." Sarah handed him a sheet of paper. "I put a star by the names of the two women who left at the same time. Only one person on the list is at work right now, Jason Aldridge. He's in Fragrance on the first floor.

Hal tucked the list into his notebook. "Thank you very much for your cooperation, Ms. Hepworth." He smiled.

"If there's anything else we can do, let us know." Sarah watched Detective Lund walk toward the elevator. "I certainly hope she's all right."

Hal pushed the button to go down and turned to Sarah. "So do we. Thanks again."

*   *   *

Jim sat on a bench in front of Feldman's where he was told to meet Hal. Stuffing the last bite of a hot dog into his mouth, he wiped the mustard from his face and crumpled up the napkin. He cocked his wrist and took careful aim at the garbage can ten feet away. The napkin flew, hit the top of the can, and fell to the ground. Grumbling, he walked over and picked it up. A gum wrapper zipped past Jim's face and into the can.

"It's all in the follow through." Hal grinned as he walked toward Jim. "Any luck?"

"I checked him out. He's got a clean record. He owns a small construction company. He's in Logan on a job, been there since Wednesday. His secretary told me he'd be back tomorrow afternoon. What did you find out?"

"She seemed to be fine when she left here Tuesday afternoon. Didn't mention leaving town to her boss, but that doesn't mean much." Hal held the door for Jim as the two walked out from the mall and into the parking lot. "Feel like a ride to Park City?"

"Sure. The canyon's beautiful this time of year." Jim got in the car and rolled his window down. Resting his elbow on the doorframe, he turned to Hal. "You wanna stop and get you something to eat? You took awhile in there, so I went ahead and grabbed a bite."

"No, I'm not hungry. Do you want to call us in?" It was more a command than a question.

"Dispatch, this is unit thirty-one."

"Go ahead thirty-one."

"We are 10-17 to Park City on a 10-69, code six. Would you inform Lieutenant Bonner and tell him we will call in from Park City?"

"10-4, thirty-one."

"We need a plate number on a late-model Toyota registered to an Elizabeth Harrison, 1746 Lakecrest, Salt Lake City, or possibly Craig Harrison of the same address." Jim rolled his window up as Hal pulled onto I-215. The two rode in silence while waiting for dispatch to get back with them.

"Thirty-one, I have a 1992 Toyota Camry registered to Elizabeth Connor Harrison, Utah plate number Romeo—delta—tango, four—one—one—two."

"10-4. Thanks."

"Did you watch the Chiefs' game Monday night?" Jim looked to Hal for an answer as he popped a Lifesaver in his mouth.

"Naw. Jean's sister's in the hospital, so we took dinner over to Bert and the kids."

"They lose their first three games, Oilers beat 'em thirty to nothin' last week, then all of a sudden they remember how to play football when they're playin' my team. It was pathetic! They beat 'em fifteen to seven." Jim shook his head in disgust. "You should come over Monday and watch the game on the big screen. The Steelers are playin'."

"Yeah, sounds good." Hal was obviously preoccupied with something else.

Jim watched the traffic around them for a while, then made another attempt at conversation. "Arlene was always wanting me to take her to Park City for the weekend. I'd say to her, 'what for?' and she'd say 'to relax and get away from the kids.' I told her we could send the kids to her mother's and relax at home. I don't get women, Hal. I just don't get 'em."

"Maybe that's why you're divorced, buddy." Hal laughed.

"Yeah, well, I'm better off." Jim looked out the window at the brightly colored leaves that adorned the steep mountain slopes towering over either side of the highway. "Jean ever bug you to take her places?"

"We get away when we can. We go out to Evanston for the horse races once or twice a year. We don't take vacations like we did when the kids were younger, though."

Hal pulled off I-80 onto the exit ramp that led to Park City. Jim nudged Hal's arm. "Do you mind stopping here?" he said, pointing at the McDonald's just off the exit. "I gotta take a leak."

They pulled into the parking lot, and Jim pulled himself from the car. "You want anything?" He leaned his head back into the car and looked at Hal.

"No, thanks." Hal sat looking over the steering wheel at the traffic going into town. Helen Connor had looked familiar to him. He searched his memory, trying to place her, but could not. He reached into his pocket and pulled out the now half-empty pack of Winstons.

Jim returned and settled into the car. "Well, where we gonna start?" He sucked down a good portion of a chocolate shake.

"There's a Days Inn up here on the left. Might as well start there," Hal said casually. His nonchalant attitude belied his love of calling the shots.

Harold Lund had been on the force for twenty-six years. He got on after spending three years as a guard at the state prison. He had tired quickly of "baby-sitting" criminals who had made the mistake of getting caught, and turned to the force, where he could capitalize on those mistakes and maybe make a difference. A lot had happened in those twenty-six years—four kids, five grandchildren, two new houses, two knee surgeries, four attempts at kicking the habit—but only one promotion. Now, Sergeant Lund was no longer preoccupied with making a difference, but rather making it to retirement. In Salt Lake City, it was not so much a matter of surviving in his line of work, but more of surviving his line of work and, for Hal, the incredibly slow passage of time.

*   *   *

Hal stepped out into the cool fall air from the lobby of the Olympic Hotel and reached in his pocket for a cigarette. He had been in seven hotels in the last hour, every one the same; only the color schemes of the decor seemed to change.

Jim trudged up the sloping sidewalk from the Regency across the street. "Any luck?" Hal called out to him as he fruitlessly searched his pockets for a lighter. "Shit!" He took the unlit cigarette from his mouth and tossed it to the ground.

Jim wiped the sweat from his forehead as he wheezed from the exertion. "Nothing at the Regency," he stopped to breathe, "but there's a white Toyota in the parking lot of the Silver Peak down the street." He looked over his shoulder at the bantam slope he had scaled. "Whew, I'm outa shape."

"Well, that's a news flash, big guy!" Hal gave Jim a friendly pat on the shoulder and headed to the car. "Let's check it out."

Hal pulled into the Silver Peak parking lot and followed Jim's directions to the far southwest corner. There was a 1992 white Toyota Camry, Utah license plate RDT 4112. "Bingo!" Hal smiled, pulled up next to the car, and shut off the engine. "Guess she just wasn't ready to come home yet."

"Yeah, that's probably the boyfriend's car over there," Jim said, stepping from the car and pointing at a red Camaro. "What a waste of our time, chasin' some slut that's entertaining her boyfriends on her husband's money."

Hal bent down with his hand and face to the window of the Toyota. "Her boyfriend must be buying. Looks like her purse is on the floor of the car." He reached down and tried the door handle. It was unlocked. Hal opened the door and looked in. The keys dangled in the ignition. "Let's go see if she's checked in." He shut the door and headed toward the hotel with Jim following behind.

Jim was eight years younger than his partner, but his balding head and round figure made him look much older than his forty-two years. He had made detective seven years and eighty pounds earlier. At one time, he had dreamed of becoming chief some day; but that was when Arlene still believed in him, when he still believed in himself. His beliefs were much simpler now: that Denver will someday own the Super Bowl title, that lasagna is a staple of life, and that nothing lasts forever.

Hal took his badge and the two photos Mrs. Connor had given them out of his pocket and showed them to the desk clerk. "We're looking for this woman," he pointed at Elizabeth in the picture. "Her car is out in the parking lot. We believe she may have checked in under an assumed name or possibly with another person."

"Would that be today?" The young man seemed nervous.

"Probably earlier in the week, maybe Tuesday," Hal replied.

"Let me get the manager to help you, sir." With that, the desk clerk slipped into a back room. Hal drummed his knuckles on the desk and scanned the spacious lobby.

"Hey!" Jim picked up a book of matches from a bowl that sat on a table near the front desk and tossed them to his partner.

"Thanks!" Hal smiled and stuck the matches in his jacket pocket.

"Hi, I'm Jeff Clayson, the manager here at the Silver Peak. How can we help you?" The tall, lanky gentleman extended his hand across the counter to Hal.

"Sergeant Lund, Salt Lake PD." Hal shook Mr. Clayson's hand. "We're trying to locate this woman," he said, holding up the picture he had shown to the desk clerk. "Her name is Elizabeth Harrison. We're wondering if she might have checked in with someone else or under another name."

It was Friday, and like everywhere else in Park City, the hotel lobby was becoming crowded. A small group had gathered at the front desk and were watching the officers' verbal exchange with the manager. Mr. Clayson quickly ushered the two men into the office and began going over the hotel registry. He explained to Hal and Jim that the Silver Peak was a time-share resort, and a membership was required in order to obtain reservations. Elizabeth Harrison was not listed as a member. Hal took down the names of the thirteen guests who had checked in Tuesday. There were only four guests who had arrived that day who had not checked out earlier in the week.

Jim conducted a room-to-room search of the possibilities they had come up with, while Hal interviewed various employees. The next hour was spent calling several guests who had lodged there during the week. At the end of it all, both men were convinced: Elizabeth Harrison had never checked into the Silver Peak Hotel.

CHAPTER 2

Sunlight pierced the gap in the vertical blinds that hung in Jeni's bedroom window. This was only the third night she had spent in her new house, and the large picture windows that afforded a breathtaking view and a great deal of light were something that would take some getting used to. She rolled over and glanced at the alarm clock. Seven fifty-six a.m. She rolled back onto her stomach and tossed the blankets up over her head in an attempt to block the invading sun. After several minutes of tossing and turning, she surrendered and threw back the covers.

Donning a white terry cloth robe, she made her way through the maze of boxes and jogged down the steps to the kitchen. She looked over the selection of coffee beans she had in the freezer and settled upon the French vanilla. Her next chore was to retrieve the Sunday *Tribune* from her back porch.

The summer had been long and hot, but the days were rapidly growing cooler as September neared its end. A fresh breeze rushed through the door as Jeni

stepped out onto the porch. She glanced across the
street at the cemetery and stood for a moment watching
the wind toss the leaves about, giving them the appearance of dancing upon the graves of the dead. The
neighborhood was quiet. Jeni breathed out a contented
sigh, pleased with the peaceful contrast to the bustling
apartment complex and crime-ridden neighborhood she
had left behind. For the first time in several months, the
anxiety Jeni had felt over the purchase of this house was
beginning to ease.

The smell of coffee floated through the air and
greeted Jeni as she walked into the house. After fixing
herself a steaming cup with just the slightest hint of
Sweet'n Low, she settled onto the couch and curled her
feet up underneath her.

Sunday was the one day each week that Jeni could
indulge herself by relaxing and reading the morning
paper instead of rushing off to work. Usually it was
afternoon, and sometimes late evening, before she was
able to sit down with the paper. But Sundays were hers,
and she could think of no better way to spend them than
sleeping late and leisurely reading the paper over a cup
of coffee.

Jeni read the front-page section practically from
cover to cover, then scanned through the world section,
reading only the headlines. She opened the local section
and a picture in the lower left-hand corner caught her
eye. She looked closely at the picture, knowing she had
seen the smiling woman before. She read the headline

next to the photo. "Salt Lake Woman Missing." She began reading the article.

"Elizabeth Harrison, 27, was reported missing on Friday." Jeni stopped reading. Elizabeth Harrison had met with her on Monday. Jeni was the attorney handling her divorce. She read on.

"Police officers discovered her car at a Park City resort but have found no leads as to her whereabouts. Mrs. Harrison told relatives she had gone to Park City for a short stay; however, she had not registered as a guest of the resort where her vehicle was found. Mrs. Harrison was due to return Thursday and has not been heard from since leaving work last Tuesday. She was last seen in Midvale late Tuesday afternoon. She was wearing a blue skirt and jacket and a white blouse. She is five feet six inches tall, medium build, and has light brown hair. If you have any information regarding Mrs. Harrison or have seen her, please contact the Salt Lake City Police Department."

Jeni read the article twice. She put the paper down and closed her eyes, trying to remember the details of her conversation with Elizabeth Harrison. She remembered how quiet the woman had been. She had seemed a little nervous, but most people were when about to file for a divorce.

One thing had disturbed Jeni about their meeting. The minor problems Elizabeth claimed as the basis for her separation from her husband seemed not only trivial, but inconsistent with her description of their relationship. When Jeni had verbalized her doubts, Elizabeth had become almost defensive, insisting only that a divorce would be in their best interest, and in the best interest of their four-year-old child.

Mrs. Harrison had asked Jeni to represent both her and her husband, Craig, saying the divorce was amicable. She had been very polite and succinct in answering Jeni's questions. In that brief meeting with Elizabeth, Jeni had learned that custody was undisputed, no alimony would be sought by either party, and division of the couples' assets had heretofore been agreed upon. Basically, this divorce would be a cakewalk for Jeni. She was mediating so many difficult cases that the ease and refreshing lack of mutual contempt and anger of the Harrisons' divorce was appealing. Theirs was not a lurid tale of infidelity, abuse, vengeance or jealous accusations. Instead, Elizabeth had painted a picture of a love that had lost its passion, its motivation, but not its bond nor its friendship. Still, something in Elizabeth Harrison's demeanor had told Jeni that she was not getting the whole story.

Jeni shook the thoughts of Elizabeth Harrison from her head and turned her attention back to the newspaper that lay open on her lap. She rarely read the classified ads, but today she thumbed through them with good reason. She ran her finger up and down the columns until it landed upon the ad she was looking for. It read: "Jenifer Sullivan, Atty. at Law. Divorce, custody, adoption. Reasonable rates." She cringed when she saw it in print, sandwiched between an ad for bankruptcy and one for an injury lawyer. The first promoted their services by using the word "cheap" and the latter by proclaiming an injured person's right to compensation. Dollar signs encircled the ad. She wondered if she had done the right thing by placing her ad. Now that she was in private practice she had to get her name out; but after seeing her ad, she was not sure this was a wise method for doing so.

It had become habit for Jeni to read the editorial section last. Depending upon their content, the opinions expressed had varied effects on her mood. They gave her food for thought for the day or, at the very least, a reason for vigorous exercise.

The public forum segment was brimming with letters of varied subjects. Jeni read with little interest a letter from a business owner, regarding the building of the new baseball stadium downtown and its effects on the area. Following that were two letters touting the importance of prayer in school and admonishing the ACLU for trying to prevent it.

Of the remaining letters, one in particular intrigued Jeni. It was from a mother of six children who was putting out a "call to action to every decent, principled, God-loving Christian," asking them to "battle against abortion and show the Lord their support by turning out to protest local abortion clinics." The letter epitomized the closed-mindedness of some of Utah's citizens and their attempt to justify their opinions and actions by purporting to have them and do them in God's name.

Reading letters of that sort made Jeni appreciate the way she had been raised. Her parents, though very

committed to the Mormon Church, had taught Jeni
tolerance of others and respect for their rights and their
choices. In the small town where Jeni had grown up,
tolerance was all too scarce. Religion there was not so
much a matter of personal conviction as it was a matter
of social acceptance.

Jeni had a great deal of respect for her parents and
their devotion to their religion. They lived the way the
leaders of the Mormon Church encouraged them to.
But, unlike many others in their community, they did not
boast of their worthy actions or use them to obtain
favorable public opinion. They quietly lived their lives
doing what they felt was right and allowing others to
make that choice for themselves.

At times, Jeni felt guilt over the fact that she was
not an active member of the church nor, for that matter,
cared to be. She had long believed that religion was
something within a person, not an organization they
belonged to. She did not consider herself a non-
religious person, as many did, but rather a nonpartisan
worshiper of a higher being. Jeni knew that her lack of
a testimony of the LDS Church would always haunt her
in some way, causing her to feel as though she had
disappointed her parents and failed to uphold the values
they had taught her. Jeni allowed herself only a moment
of guilt before trotting up the stairs and running a hot
bath.

She eased her way into the steaming hot water
slowly after testing it with her toe. Every muscle in her
body relaxed as the heat soothed them.

Thoughts of her family stirred a longing for home that she had not felt for a while. The purchase of a new house, the refurbishing it had required, and struggling to survive her transition into private practice had made it difficult to feel anything but overwhelmed. She toyed with the idea of making the two-hour round trip to her parents' house, but then, realizing she still had dictation to catch up on, decided against it. Instead, she picked up the cordless phone that rested on the hamper next to the tub and dialed their number.

"Hello?" Her mother answered on the first ring.

"Hi, Mom!"

"Hey, Jen! How are you, honey?" Her voice was pleasant and soothing.

"Good. Tired, but good. How are you and Dad?"

"Fine as ever. When do we get to come up and see the house now that you've moved in? I'm sure it looks a lot different than it did when we saw it."

"Actually, Mom, it doesn't look much better. The work's all done, but I've got boxes and furniture scattered everywhere. Hopefully, I'll have it organized by next weekend. Maybe you could come up then. I'll fix dinner."

"Hey, can't beat that."

"Mom, you've experienced my cooking. It can definitely be beat."

"Oh, you're too hard on yourself. Do you need any help?" She went on without waiting for a reply. "Dad and I could come up this week and help you get things straightened around."

"No, thanks, Mom. My schedule is pretty hectic. Besides, I want you to come up and relax, not work."

Jeni talked her mother out of coming up during the week and into coming up for dinner on Saturday. They talked for a while about the family, and Jeni talked about work. Their conversation was not lengthy, but Jeni felt much better as she hung up. She placed the cordless phone on the hamper and enjoyed the comfort and repose the bubble bath offered.

After a breakfast of bagels and fruit, Jeni settled herself behind the desk in her office, the one room in the house that was organized and put away. She took a stack of files from her briefcase and placed them on her desk. She tested the tape recorder and put in a new tape. The second file she took from the stack was that of Elizabeth Harrison's divorce case. Jeni opened it up and read through the notes she had made. The article that had declared Mrs. Harrison missing resurfaced in Jeni's mind. She had an appointment with the Harrisons scheduled for Wednesday. She could not help but wonder if they both would be there. She dictated instructions on preparing the file into the recorder; the papers would be drawn up by Wednesday. As she completed dictation on the file, she gazed out the window and viewed the sprawling city. She wondered if Mrs. Harrison were out there somewhere among the concrete maze.

CHAPTER 3

"It looks pretty damn good, if I say so myself," Hal said as he stepped back and looked over his handiwork with a grin. "Pretty damn good."

Steve smiled as he buffed the last few tiles. "Yeah, we didn't do too bad."

"Hand me that putty knife, would ya?" Hal reached out his hand and waited for his son to place the knife in it. He gathered up his tools, separating them from Steve's, and put them in a battered blue toolbox.

"You want to stay and watch the game?"

"Sure, if I can talk you out of another beer." Hal set his toolbox on the bathroom counter and washed the glue and caulking from his hands. "Who's playing?"

"I'm not sure." Steve walked out and returned quickly with a Coors Light in each hand. "You think Shelly and Mom have caught each other up on all the gossip yet?" He grinned and offered one of the beers to his father.

Hal dried his hands and took the can from Steve. "They've probably only scratched the surface." He looked at his watch. "Let's see, Shelly's been over there for about three hours. That means they've talked about us, they've talked about the rest of the family, and now they're moving on to friends and neighbors. By the time the game's over, they'll be catching up on the latest word on their favorite soap stars." Hal put his arm around Steve's shoulder as they walked toward the living room.

Steve grabbed the remote and settled onto the couch. He turned on the set and found the game, then turned to Hal. "Thanks for your help, Dad. I really appreciate it."

Hal grinned. "No problem. Just give me a few weeks before you decide to take on the upstairs bathroom."

Hal and Steve exchanged stories and discussed their jobs as the game played in the background. Steve was telling his dad about the anniversary present he was planning to buy Shelly. Hal battled within himself as he listened, wanting so much to talk to Steve about the doubts he had been plagued with, about the fantasies he was beginning to have, about the coldness with which he was beginning to view the world, but silence won. After all, this was his son. Hal pushed the thoughts from his mind. The two of them were talking over the possibility of going golfing the following week when the phone rang.

"Dad, it's for you." Steve stuck his head around the corner from the kitchen.

"Your mom?" Hal asked as he walked toward the phone.

"No. I don't know who it is."

Hal took the receiver from Steve. "Hello?"

"Hal, sorry to bother you. Jean told me I'd find you over there."

Hal recognized Merril Bonner's voice. He grew concerned, knowing his Lieutenant wouldn't track him down on a Sunday unless it were something important.

"No problem. What's up?"

"We've got a body up Emigration Canyon. We think it might be your missing person."

Hal grabbed a pencil and scribbled the needed information on an envelope he found on the kitchen table. He apologized to his son for running off and headed for Emigration Canyon.

Traffic was light. A tourist arriving or passing through on a typical Sunday would never believe that this was a metropolitan area housing over a million people. It was like a huge playground at a school that had closed for the summer, with only a few trespassing youth on its grounds.

Hal drove his Blazer up Eighth South and hoped it was not Elizabeth Harrison they had found, but something was telling him that it was. He experienced a twinge of guilt over the excitement he suddenly felt at the prospect of a homicide case. He had only worked on two other homicides this year, and his involvement had been minimal. He had not headed a murder investigation since the Archuleta case three years ago. Those unwanted memories caused Hal's conscience to wince. He wanted a chance to redeem himself with

Captain Jarvis, and maybe this would be it. His adrenalin began pumping, and the needle of the speedometer rose steadily with his pulse. He sucked on a Wintergreen Lifesaver, trying to mask the smell of beer on his breath.

He slowed down as he passed Camp Kostopulos and looked for a turnoff to the right. About three-quarters of a mile past the camp, he saw a dirt road and a sign that read "Emigration Heights, Lots Still Available, Build to Suit, Abbot Construction." As Hal pulled off onto the muddy thoroughfare, he stopped and jotted down the phone numbers from the sign. Ahead of him were two squad cars and a half-dozen other vehicles huddled around a large, mucky area. Hal recognized his partner's dark green Cutlass and pulled up beside it. He reached behind his seat and grabbed a dark blue ball cap with "Police" written boldly across it in gold lettering. He pulled the hat over his sandy-blond hair and walked toward his partner.

Jim stood with a gathering of officers, his hands tucked deep into the pockets of his baggy, faded jeans. He looked up at Hal and nodded in greeting. "What took you so long, Tex?"

"I was at Steve's. They had to track me down." Hal surveyed the scene as he neared the other officers. "What've we got?"

"Over here." John Meacham led Hal twenty yards down a slight embankment to the edge of a thicket. Hal had gone through the academy with John, and the two had worked together as patrol officers in the seventies.

John was a lieutenant with the county sheriff's department now, and one of the officers Hal respected most. "Some kid was up here four wheelin' and found her."

The stench was familiar. Hal had become immune to its nauseating affects, but he would never become accustomed to the sight of a murder victim's corpse. Hal bent over the body, studying every detail. The woman's head was caked with black soil, making it hard to discern the color of her shoulder-length hair. Her clothing was in disarray, but there were no signs of rips or tears. She was wearing a white Duke University sweatshirt and dark blue jeans. On the ring finger of her left hand was a good-sized diamond.

"Think it could be your missing person?" John looked to Hal for an answer.

"Could be. Fits the description. No ID, huh?"

John shook his head. "No."

"Is this how she was found?" Hal took a cigarette from the pocket of his blue T-shirt and lit it. He tossed the used match into the mud, then thinking better of it, stooped to pick it up. About eight inches from his hand was a white button. He made a mental note of it.

"She was face down, like this." John motioned with his hand to show how she had been turned over. "Whoever left her here must have been in a hurry. She wasn't buried, easily could have been. And it wouldn't have taken much more effort to dump the body behind the bitterbrush here." John pointed to the dense shrubs next to the woman's body.

Hal scanned the lifeless body for signs of trauma, then turned to John. "Any idea on cause of death?"

"Looks as though there were several blows to the back of the head."

"Has the coroner been called?"

"He should be here within the half-hour," John answered.

John and Hal looked toward a county patrol officer who approached from the convocation of policemen. "Dispatch just got back with us." The officer spoke directly to John. "We're supposed to turn it over to SLPD." He looked at Hal.

"It's all yours, Hal." John placed a hand on Hal's shoulder. "Count on our cooperation." With that, John walked back toward his vehicle, accompanied by the young officer.

Hal signaled to Jim and yelled out as his partner approached. "Let's seal it off."

"Gotcha!" Jim called out in compliance. He turned around and carried the instructions to the uniformed officers from his department. As one of the officers joined Hal, he picked up the white button and placed it in one of the clear plastic bags the officer had brought with him.

"I don't want one shred of evidence passed over. Turn over every blade of grass if you have to."

Hal looked over the area immediately surrounding the body, looking for any sign of evidence. He then scanned the area around him. The previous day's rain had turned the future construction site into a disheveled mire. The musty smell of damp leaves and the cool fall air reminded Hal of hunting deer with his father and later with his sons. The memories that came to him were pleasant, ones he had always cherished. He thought of the beautiful terrain they had hiked through, the jokes and laughter he and his brothers, his father and his sons had shared. The excitement of seeing a big buck, the thrill of tracking and slaying the animal. He suddenly wondered if the woman whose body lay at his feet was the random prey of a hunter of a different sort, a maniacal being driven by a lust for the thrill of taking a victim.

                           *   *   *

Merril Bonner met Hal and Jim as they walked into the station. "What a way to spend a Sunday afternoon, huh? Sorry, boys," the lieutenant apologized. "Well, what did we find out?" He walked with them down the long hallway that led to the detective division.

"We're pretty sure it's the Harrison woman. Her husband is meeting us here, and we're going down to see if he can identify the body," Hal answered Lieutenant Bonner's question.

"Have you questioned him yet?" Bonner asked.

"Yeah." Hal held the door to the office for the other two men. "We paid him a visit last night. He said he hadn't seen his wife since last Monday. He denied arguing with her, but they usually do. He seemed rather uptight. Couldn't tell if it was nerves or concern."

"He was scared shitless, if you want my opinion," Jim spoke up. "Guess he has a reason to be, now."

The three men sat down in Lieutenant Bonner's office and discussed how the questioning of Craig Harrison should proceed. They knew they had to be careful of what they asked him because they were not prepared to file any charges.

The intercom on Bonner's desk sounded. "There's a Mr. Harrison here at the front desk to see Hal."

"Thanks. He'll be right down to get him." Bonner looked up at Hal and Jim. "Handle him carefully, but make sure he knows not to leave town."

Hal and Jim walked back down the corridor and turned the corner. Craig Harrison stood next to the reception desk. He was dressed in blue jeans and a buttoned cotton shirt. He nervously ran his fingers through the thick shock of black curls that framed his brow.

"Mr. Harrison?" Hal called out as they entered the reception area.

Craig turned toward them and nodded in greeting.

"Please, sit down." Hal gently nudged Craig's elbow, directing him toward a tan sofa in the corner of the room.

Craig sat down and looked at Hal.

"Mr. Harrison, we have recovered the body of a woman," Hal stumbled over the words. "We believe it may be your wife." Hal had come to believe that delivering bad news was almost as difficult as receiving it. Craig's eyes grew wide. His face remained blank as he swallowed hard.

Seeing no response from Craig, Hal continued. "I know this is difficult, but we need you to identify the body."

Craig stared down at the floor and slowly rocked back and forth on the edge of the couch. Whatever emotions he might be feeling were being suppressed.

"If you'll come with us, please." Hal stood and waited for Craig. Jim walked to the front desk and signed his name in a logbook before receiving a key to the elevator. As he rejoined Hal, Craig rose from the sofa and followed the two officers into one of three elevators. Jim placed the key in the panel and pushed the button for the lower level.

As the doors opened, Craig looked at a sign with an arrow that pointed the way to the crime lab, evidence rooms and the medical examiner's office. Hal stopped and turned to Craig. "If you would prefer to have someone with you, a family member or friend, we'll wait while you arrange for that."

Craig cleared his throat. "No," he answered in a quiet voice.

The three men walked down the wide corridor in silence. They reached a small lounge area, and Hal asked Craig to wait for a moment. Hal and Jim entered a room marked only with the number 175. Craig sat on the edge of a soft chair, wiping the perspiration from his palms onto the knees of his jeans. After a few minutes, Hal and Jim returned. Craig stood and waited for direction from one of the men.

"Mr. Harrison, we need to prepare you for what you're going to see." A balding man wearing a light blue lab coat, standing next to Jim, spoke. "The body is in the beginning stages of decomposition. It may be difficult to determine identity at first, but we'll ask that you study the body for a moment, though it may be extremely disquieting. We just want you to be sure whether or not this is your wife."

Craig nodded. "Okay."

The man led Craig, Jim and Hal through an office to a set of metal doors. When he opened the doors, a putrid odor greeted them. As they neared a stainless-steel table, the man moved to the opposite side and looked up at Hal and Jim before pulling back the white sheet that lay over the body. Hal nodded and the sheet was retracted.

Craig stared for a moment at the woman's face. Bowing his head, he brought his right hand up and gripped his forehead, shading his eyes. Hal looked at Jim, who shrugged his shoulders.

After a long moment, Craig took a deep breath and looked up at the man who stood across the table from him. "It's Liz." He looked down at his wife's lifeless body, then closed his eyes tightly, and turned away.

Hal spoke up. "Are you absolutely positive?"

"Yes," Craig nodded. "Yes, I am."

Hal motioned for the man to cover Elizabeth's body with the sheet. He then led Craig back to the lounge area. "Mr. Harrison, I'm sorry about the loss of your wife. I want you to know that we'll do everything we possibly can to ensure that the person responsible for her death is found and brought up on charges. We're going to want to talk with you in the next couple of days. We'll need to know where you're going to be and how to reach you."

"Okay."

"You might want to obtain a lawyer and have him present during our interview, for your own protection." Hal paused, not knowing how to tactfully relay his next instructions. "I would strongly suggest that you not leave town without notifying us."

Craig looked up. "Okay."

Hal and Jim escorted Craig back to the first-floor reception area and told him they would be in touch with him the following day. As they walked back toward their office, Jim turned to Hal. "He knows something."

"What do you mean?" Hal asked.

"I don't know; he just seemed funny to me. I think he knew it was her before we walked in there."

"We'll find out, won't we?" Hal smiled at Jim as he held the door. "We've got a long night ahead of us."

Jim walked over to his desk and picked up the phone. He dialed and waited for an answer, then looked over at Hal. "What do you want on your pizza?"

CHAPTER 4

After what seemed like an endless diatribe, the judge granted the divorce and his gavel fell. Jeni's client rose and shook her hand, shot a vexing glance at his now ex-wife, and quickly walked out. Jeni walked from the courtroom and headed toward the elevators.

"Hey, Sullivan!"

Jeni turned to see Brian Fisher coming from courtroom three. "Hi, Brian." Her tone was unenthusiastic.

"Those civil cases getting the best of you?" He slung a black leather satchel over his shoulder.

"They keep me busy." Jeni pushed the button and looked at the elevator impatiently.

"Well, if you ever decide you want to be a real lawyer, come on back. You can take the heat." Brian pushed his wire-frame glasses back up the slope of his nose. "Besides, Jackson's not going to be around much longer, not the way he's going."

"Are you kidding?" Jeni turned to Brian. "He's going to run for district attorney and probably win. I'm not about to work with him again, let alone for him."

The elevator doors finally opened. "Well, I just think you're being wasted on civil."

"Thanks, Brian, but I really do enjoy it." She attempted a smile as the doors closed.

Jeni had wanted to be a lawyer since the eighth grade. She had imagined a fascinating career defending underdogs, battling injustice, and conquering corruption. The picture never included the grueling hours of research she would face as a law clerk or the sexual harassment she would face as a young female attorney.

Jeni had worked through her final two years of school as a law clerk at the district attorney's office. When they offered her a position as a prosecuting attorney upon her graduation, she could not have been more thrilled. She started out in traffic court and quickly moved up to misdemeanors. By the end of her second year as a prosecutor, she was taking felony cases in district court. And about that same time, Arthur Jackson began his assault on her womanhood, her dignity and, ultimately, her career.

Resisting his pathetic advances had threatened to be her ruin and had forced her to give up her position. Though Jeni left the district attorney's office, it had not been for the worse. She was becoming a respected attorney in the civil arena. Her practice was new, but coming along steadily.

Despite the ordeal Jeni had gone through, she loved her career. Some days she had to invoke those words over and over, but deep down she knew it was true.

Jeni stepped from the elevators and walked across the huge marble foyer of the courthouse. It was unusually vacant, and the sharp, staccato sound of her heels echoed in the void. As she neared the doors, a stocky man in a bailiff's uniform rushed ahead of her.

"Let me get that, Miss Sullivan." The young man grinned, exposing a row of metal braces. He opened the door and held it for Jeni.

"Thanks, Bob."

"Anytime!" He stuck his chest out in a jesting manner. "That's my job. Protect and serve."

Jeni laughed and waved as she walked away.

"Have a nice day, Miss Sullivan!" He watched her walk down the steps to the sidewalk. When Jeni was out of his range of sight, he stepped back inside the building.

The walk from the courthouse to her office was a pleasant one. A cool breeze played with Jeni's soft blonde locks, tossing them back and forth. The air was laced with the rich smell of coffee and a potpourri of food as she walked past a row of restaurants. Her brisk pace was comfortable and made the two blocks pass quickly.

"Good morning, Jeni!" Kate looked up from her desk as Jeni walked into the office.

"Good morning."

"How was your weekend?"

Jeni picked up the stack of mail that sat on the corner of her secretary's desk. "Not bad. How was yours?"

"Not long enough." Kate smiled. "Here are your messages."

"Thanks." Jeni took the pink slips of paper from Kate's hand. "Would you get Brent Robinson's file and write up a bill?"

"Sure."

"Thanks." Jeni walked into her office. She placed her briefcase on her desk and put the stack of mail on top of the morning newspaper that sat unopened. She thumbed through her messages and stopped when she came to one from Craig Harrison. The name grabbed Jeni's attention. If she remembered correctly, Craig was the name of the missing woman's husband. Yes, it was Craig and Elizabeth Harrison.

She looked again at the message. Only his name and phone number were written on the paper, and Kate had checked the box indicating to return his call.

"When did Craig Harrison call?" Jeni asked as she walked back to Kate's desk and handed her the message.

Kate looked at the slip of paper. "Oh, he called just after I got here, maybe quarter to nine." She handed the message back to Jeni.

"What did he say?"

"He just asked for you and said it was important that he talk with you as soon as possible." Kate looked up at Jeni over the top of her glasses.

Jeni walked back to her desk without saying anything more. She sat with her hand on the phone for a moment, then picked it up and dialed Craig Harrison's number.

"Hello?"

"Mr. Harrison?"

"Yes?"

"This is Jenifer Sullivan. I'm returning your call."
Jeni picked a pencil up from her desk and leaned back
in her chair.

"Yes. I appreciate you calling me back." Craig's
fatigue was evident in his voice.

There was a silence. Jeni prompted Craig. "What
can I do for you?"

"I need—well, I'm not sure where to start." Craig
cleared his throat. "You met with my wife, Liz, last
week. It was about our divorce."

"Yes, I remember talking with her." Jeni thought of
the article she had read in the paper and listened
intently.

"She told me you would represent both of us, and,
well, now I need your advice." Craig stumbled awkwardly over his words.

"Okay." Jeni rolled the pencil in her fingers and
waited for Craig to continue.

"I don't know if you've heard about what happened,
but . . ."

"I read about your wife in the paper." Jeni found
herself atypically at a loss for words.

"Ryan, my son, is with her mother. When I found
out about Liz last night, I went to get him." Craig shook
his head. "She wouldn't let me near him. Wouldn't
even let me in the house. I don't know what my legal

rights are, I—I just want my son." Craig's voice cracked with emotion.

"So your wife is still missing?" There was a long silence. "Mr. Harrison?"

"No. I thought you knew."

"I'm sorry. You thought I knew what?"

"Her body was found yesterday." The words rolled off Craig's tongue and landed like a lead weight in Jeni's ear.

Jeni struggled to collect her thoughts. "I'm very sorry, Mr. Harrison."

"Please, please just help me get Ryan back."

"Mr. Harrison, is there any way you could meet with me this afternoon?"

"Yes. What time?"

Jeni looked at her schedule. Only her lunch hour was free. "Would twelve-thirty be all right?"

"Yes, fine. Where is your office?"

"It's at 448 South 400 East, Suite B, downstairs."

"Okay. I'll be there at twelve-thirty."

Jeni again offered her sympathies before hanging up. She put the receiver down slowly. Her eye caught the newspaper that lay beneath the morning's mail. She unfolded the paper and removed the local section. There on the first page were the headlines: "Woman's Body Found.'" The article told of Elizabeth Harrison's body being found in Emigration Canyon but gave few details. Police had declined to give the cause of death, saying only that suspicious circumstances indicated foul play.

Jeni's mind went over the multitude of scenarios that might have taken place. Her curiosity was piqued, and though up to this point her involvement with the Harrisons had been minimal, she suddenly felt the need to know what had happened to Elizabeth.

"Jeni?" Kate poked her head around the door.

Jeni folded the paper and put it to the back of her desk. "Yes."

"Your ten-thirty appointment is here." She looked to Jeni for instructions.

Jeni began clearing her desk. "Thanks Kate. Go ahead and send them in."

*   *   *

The door to her office opened, and Jeni looked up from the book she had been pouring over to find Kate peeking in. "Hey, I'm going for some lunch. Do you want anything?"

"Where are you going?"

"I thought I'd get a sandwich from Lloyd's." Kate motioned in the direction of the deli down the street.

Jeni reached for her briefcase. "Yeah, could you pick me up a salad?" She retrieved a ten-dollar bill from her daily planner and rose to hand it to Kate.

"What kind?" Kate tucked the bill into the pocket of her sweater.

"Just their garden salad. Thanks."

"Be right back." Kate walked out, leaving Jeni's door ajar.

Jeni turned her attention back to the book of Utah Codes she had been engrossed in. She went back and forth between the pages, jotting notes as she read.

"Excuse me."

Jeni looked up, startled by the sudden interruption. A dark, good-looking man stood in her office doorway. He wore navy blue Dockers and a blue and tan rugby shirt that hung nicely on his tall, athletic frame. Jeni stood. "Can I help you?"

"Yes, I'm Craig Harrison." He turned back toward the reception area and motioned. "There wasn't anyone out here, so . . ." He hesitated.

"My secretary went to lunch," Jeni explained as she walked toward Craig. "Please come in." Jeni shook his hand and showed him to a black leather chair that faced her desk.

Jeni glanced at the clock as she walked behind the desk. It was twenty-five minutes after twelve. She smiled to herself. She had grown appreciative of clients who were prompt.

"What can I do for you, Mr. Harrison?"

"I just don't know where to turn." Craig fidgeted in his seat. "I don't know what my rights are or how to go about dealing with my mother-in-law." Craig's expression was solemn, but his deep brown eyes were like those of a frightened child.

"Okay. Is there or has there ever been a restraining order against you?"

"You mean that I can't see my son?" Craig asked, clarifying the question. "No."

"Your son, or your wife."

"No, not ever."

"Good. Now, I discussed your relationship briefly with your wife, but I'd like you to tell me about it, if you will." Jeni pressed her fingers together and looked intently at Craig.

"Well, we've known each other since childhood. She grew up down the street and was my sister's best friend all through school. We dated after she graduated from high school and got married about a year later."

"How would you describe your relationship?" Jeni prompted.

"It was good in some ways, bad in others." Craig shrugged his shoulders.

Jeni looked at the distress in Craig's eyes and felt a twinge of guilt at asking these questions. "Elizabeth told me you had agreed upon custody and care of your son. She said you would share custody, but that he would live with her. Is that correct?"

"Yes, but I still have a right to my son now, don't I?" he questioned with concern.

"Of course you do. I'm just trying to establish the situation so that my actions will be knowledgeable and appropriate." Jeni reached for a pen. "What is your relationship with your mother-in-law like?"

"It's not good. It never has been."

"Was she close to your wife?" Jeni's hand was poised on a notepad.

"No, not at all. Liz and her mom never got along, even when she was younger. Helen is a very different lady. She would hardly talk to Liz before Ryan was born. I guess they were closer after that, but it was all because of Ryan. That's the only thing that they had in common, really."

"Does she tend Ryan often?"

"No." Craig shook his head. "She'll go get Ryan and take him to the park and stuff like that, but Liz rarely had her tend."

"What did she say to you last night?"

"She told me I'd never see my son again, and she shut the door. That was it. She wouldn't answer the door or the phone after that." The emotion was beginning to show on Craig's face.

"What's your mother-in-law's name and address?" Jeni wrote the information down as Craig gave it to her. She picked up the phone and spoke to Craig as she dialed. "I'm calling the Division of Family Services. We'll get them to give a decree on temporary custody."

Jeni leaned back in her chair and waited for an answer. "Yes, may I speak with Barbara Giles, please?" She spoke to the woman, with whom she was obviously well-acquainted. Craig listened as Jeni explained the situation, then glanced out the window that offered a view of passing pedestrians and the traffic on Fourth South.

Jeni finished speaking with the woman and put down the receiver. "She's taking up the case for us on that end. Custody is automatically yours. What we're doing is involving DFS for our own protection." Jeni began writing as she spoke. "Mrs. Giles will take you and an officer of the court to your mother-in-law's house to get your son." Jeni handed Craig the paper. "Here's her address. Call me as soon as you get back, and we'll go from there."

Craig stood and read the directions before placing the paper in his pocket. "Thank you." He stuck his hand across Jeni's desk as she rose.

"This doesn't mean that it's over." Jeni shook the hand Craig had offered her. "It all depends on your mother-in-law. We might have to go before the judge and get an injunction if she refuses to cooperate."

Craig nodded in understanding. "Can I go over there now?"

"Yes. Mrs. Giles will be waiting for you." Jeni walked Craig to the door. "I'll be in my office all afternoon. Give me a call."

"Thanks again." Craig attempted a smile as he left.

Kate walked through the door Craig held open. "Thank you." She put one brown paper bag on her desk and handed the other one to Jeni. "Did you have a twelve-thirty, or was that a lunch date?" She raised her eyebrows.

"Don't get your hopes up; he's a client." Jeni smiled and shook her head.

Kate walked outside the office again and returned with two sodas. "We'll get you married off someday." Kate handed a Diet Coke to Jeni.

"Thanks." She looked at the clock behind Kate's desk. "I've got ten minutes to enjoy this. Would you get

Brenda Vigil's file out and bring it to me before she arrives?"

"You bet."

Jeni took the salad into her office and closed the door.

CHAPTER 5

"You look like hell!" Jim watched his partner walk past him to his desk.

"Thanks. Good to see you, too." Hal sat down and took the lid from a styrofoam cup containing coffee.

"You get any sleep last night?" Jim lumbered over.

"Very little. How about you?"

"Slept like a baby." Jim sat on a vacant desk next to Hal's. "What've you got planned for us?"

"I thought we'd hit the neighborhood first, talk to everyone we possibly can. Then we can hit the mall, find out if anyone else saw her leave Tuesday, and get a statement from the woman we talked with last night."

Jim nodded.

"Then we'll take another trip to Park City, see if we can find anyone who saw her there." Hal gulped his coffee.

"Okay. We gonna talk to the husband today?"

"Probably. I want to talk with her mother again, first. I want to find out who her friends were and talk to them. The paperwork should be in order sometime this afternoon, and we'll search the house." Hal filed through the papers on his desk, looking for the list of employees Sarah Hepworth had given him. Finding it, he grabbed a pen and circled the names of those he had been unable to reach by phone the night before. He drained the last of the coffee and stood. "Let's go."

                    *   *   *

Hal got out of the car and tossed his spent cigarette to the ground. Jim walked around from his side of the car to join him. "You take that street," Hal said, pointing at the street the bordered the south side of the Harrison's home. "I'll take this street."

"All right."

"Get everything you can. Ask if they saw anything Tuesday or if they've noticed anything suspicious. Find out how they felt about the Harrisons and if they noticed patterns, like when they came and went."

"Okay. Meet you back here?" Jim waited for Hal to nod before crossing the street and heading to the house behind the Harrisons'.

Hal tucked his leather-bound notebook under his arm and knocked on the door of the house just north of Elizabeth's. An elderly woman wearing a peach-colored housedress answered the door.

"Yes?"

"Ma'am, I'm Sergeant Lund, with the Salt Lake Police Department." Hal held up his identification for the woman to view. "I'd like to ask you a few questions about your neighbor, Elizabeth Harrison." The woman opened the screen door, and Hal followed her into the house.

"It's a shame what happened to her." The woman walked slowly over to a chair and sat down. "Sit, sit." She motioned to the couch nearby. "She was such a sweet girl. I'm not in the best of health, you know, and she looked out for me. I've been alone now for eight years. Charles died in '85. He had a stroke in '83. He was never the same after that. He could still function and all, he just was never the same. Kind of gave up his will, you know? Anyway, she's been such a help. She'd take me down to Smith's every Wednesday to get my groceries. I don't drive, you know. Just a sweet girl."

"When was the last time you saw her?" Hal opened his notebook.

"Oh, let's see, she watered the lawn Monday. No, no—that was Sunday. She took care of my lawn, you know. In the winter, her husband would shovel my walks. Last winter, he was out of town working and it snowed, oh, probably a foot, and she was over here shoveling. Bless her heart. She did her walks and all of mine."

"What was her husband like?"

"Oh, he's a nice fellow. Didn't say much. I broke a hip in May. He came over and moved my furniture around, so it would be easier for me to get to things. He had everything set up so I could get along by myself. She brought me dinner every night for nearly three weeks. Not much of a cook, God bless her." The

woman chuckled, and dabbed the moisture from her eye.
"She was a sweet girl."

"You say she took you shopping every Wednesday?"

"Yes. I like going down on Wednesday because it's
not as crowded, and the bakery goods are always fresh.
I don't like going down on Fridays or weekends. It gets
so busy and with all the kids running around it's enough
to drive me crazy."

"Did she tell you she would be out of town last
Wednesday?" Hal asked, hoping for a brief reply.

"No. I had to call my nephew to get my groceries
Thursday. He's so busy that I hate to bother him and
all, but I didn't know how else I was going to get to the
store. My nephew is really the only family I have left in
the area. My son moved to St. George two years ago.
Tried to talk me into it, too. But I've lived here my
whole life, and I'm not about to move now. Makes me
tired to think about living down there. My oldest
daughter lives in Phoenix, and my younger one's back in
Michigan."

Hal jumped in when the woman paused. "Has she
left town without telling you before?"

"Oh, yes. It's not like she had to report to me or
anything. She didn't leave a lot. They went to California over the summer, but she told me then they'd be
gone for a week. In fact," she rose from her chair with
a groan and continued, "she brought me back this little
seashell." She walked over to a shelf cluttered with
knick-knacks and picked up a lacquered conch shell.

"She was so thoughtful." She spoke as she handed the shell to Hal. She returned to her chair with a heavy sigh.

Hal smiled gratuitously and placed the shell on an end table next to him. "Have you ever heard Elizabeth and her husband fight, or did she ever talk about them fighting?"

"No. You know, I was so surprised when he moved out. They were such a cute couple."

"So she never mentioned arguing with her husband?"

"No. You know, come to think of it, we never really talked much about her. We mostly talked about me, I guess."

Hal found that easy to believe. "Did she have friends over often?"

"Well, she had one friend that I'd see now and again, but I didn't notice a lot of people over there. Of course, I'm getting older, and I don't spend a lot of time nosing in on other people's business."

"This friend, was it a woman or a man?" Hal asked.

"A woman. She'd come over fairly often. I think maybe Elizabeth was a little like me, not wanting to stay alone, you know. Of course, I'm getting used to it now. I spend most of my time alone anymore."

Hal's patience was dwindling. "Why do you say that she didn't like staying alone?"

"Her friend would stay with her sometimes when her husband was out of town working. He wasn't gone all that often, but he left now and then."

"Do you know this friend's name?" Hal asked.

"Oh, heavens no. I guess . . ."

Hal hurled another question at the woman. "Can you describe her appearance?" he asked.

"Oh, I don't know. Short dark hair. Tall, I think. Like I say, I don't meddle. I saw her come and go now and again."

"Do you know what kind of car this friend drove?" Hal asked.

The elderly woman shook her head. "Don't know much about cars. I never even had a license myself. But I do know that it was red. More like a truck than a car, but it wasn't really a truck, either."

"Can I get your name and phone number, ma'am?"

"Thelma Johnson. William Johnson was my husband's great-grandfather. He was one of Brigham Young's bodyguards, you know. In fact . . ."

Hal cut her story short. "And your phone number?"

"It's 555-4935. When Charles and I moved to this neighborhood—oh, forty years ago—we got that number."

Hal stood and handed the woman his card. "I appreciate your help, Mrs. Johnson. If you think of anything else that might be significant, feel free to call."

"I just hope you find who did this. It's not safe out there anymore, you know? It's like I was telling my nephew on the phone the other day, we're in the last days now, and the devil's been unleashed." The woman followed Hal to the door. "While I've got you here, is there anything you can do about that dog of my neighbors?"

"Dog?" Hal was confused by the question.

"My neighbor through the block has a dog that just doesn't know when to shut up. If I get up in the night, I just have the dickens of a time getting back to sleep, you know?"

"You'd have to call animal control and report the problem to them." Hal opened the door hoping to escape quickly.

"Well, all right. I just thought since you were here—you know."

"Have a nice day, Mrs. Johnson." Hal stepped out the door and felt a wave of relief as he heard it shut behind him. He spent the next forty-five minutes talking with other neighbors and hearing over and over again that Craig and Elizabeth Harrison were model neighbors, who were very private.

Hal walked back to the car and leaned against the door. He took a Winston from his pocket and lit it with his last match. He saw Jim talking with a young woman on a porch a few houses down the street. He looked around the neighborhood, noticing that the lawns were all well trimmed. The rustling of leaves, a few birds and an occasional car were the only sounds. It reminded him of how his neighborhood used to be, before the apartment complex went in down the street.

"Hey, could you hurry it up a little?" he called out to Jim, who sauntered toward him.

Jim picked his pace up slightly. "It's pretty warm today." He loosened his tie as he walked to the passenger side of the car. "What did you get?"

Hal opened his door and talked to Jim across the top of the car. "Nothing significant. What about you?"

"Nobody saw her Tuesday. I got one woman who thinks she saw Harrison's truck there Tuesday around five." Jim got in and shut his door. "Same lady saw someone driving a new Cherokee poking around kind of suspicious-like Wednesday afternoon."

"She didn't recognize him?" Hal asked.

"Her. And no, she didn't recognize her. I got a description, though." Jim wiped a bead of sweat from his brow. "Nothin', huh?" He looked to Hal.

"Everybody I talked to seemed to like both Elizabeth and her husband." Hal spoke as he pulled away from the curb. "I talked with a Mr. Cornaby, who lives across the street from them. He seems to be the neighborhood watchdog. He keeps an eye on things, usually knows what's going on. He hasn't seen anything suspicious. He and a Mrs. Johnson gave me the description of one of her friends that they both see over there quite a bit, but neither of them knew her name."

"Tall, athletic-looking brunette?" Jim asked.

"Yeah," Hal answered.

"Yeah. One of the women I talked to said she was the only person she really noticed coming and going."

Hal rolled his window down and tossed his cigarette out. "Well, not much to go on yet. Hope we have better luck at Feldman's."

*   *   *

"Sure, I saw Liz leave. In fact, we were walking out together when she ran into some guy she knew." The young woman popped her gum between sentences.

"Can you describe him?" Hal looked up from his notes.

"He was an older guy, maybe fifty or so."

Hal winced. "Did she talk to him?"

"Yeah. He called out to her and we stopped. Then she told me to go ahead, and she walked over to talk to him." She rocked forward in her chair. "He seemed really nice."

"So that was the last you saw her? She was still in the store?" Hal glanced at the pictures that adorned the walls of Sarah Hepworth's office, which he had made into a makeshift interrogation room.

"No. I got in my car and was pulling out and saw her walking to her car."

"Was she alone?" Jim interjected. Hal shot a glance at his partner, who sat slumped in a chair to the side of him. He hated it when Jim asked a question before he could get it out.

"Yeah."

"Thank you very much, Miss Wiscombe. If you remember anything else, please contact us." Hal stood and handed her a card before opening the door for her. He looked up at Sarah Hepworth, who sat outside with a small group of people. "You can send the next one in now."

Sarah nodded to a man who looked to be in his mid to late twenties. She spoke to Hal as they approached the office. "This is Michael Poulsen."

"Mr. Poulsen, I'm Sergeant Lund, and this is Officer Webber." Hal had tired of formalities and sat without shaking the man's hand. "I'm sure you're well aware by now why we're here."

"Ye . . ." the word refused to rise from the man's throat. He coughed into his clenched fist and cleared his throat. "Excuse me. Yes."

"How well did you know Elizabeth Harrison?"

"Pretty well. We worked in the same department until I got transferred to Housewares in July."

"Did she ever discuss her personal life with you?"

"Depends on what you mean." The man brought his left foot up to rest on his right knee. "She talked about her son a lot."

"Did she ever talk about her marriage?" Hal glanced over and noticed Jim cleaning his fingernails.

"No, not really. She'd talk about like what her and her husband did, you know, when they'd go out or something."

"Did she ever lead you to believe she was unhappy in her marriage?"

"No. In fact, I didn't even know they were getting divorced 'til after all this happened."

"What shift did you work on Tuesday?" Hal searched the paper before him for the answer.

"Eleven to seven."

"Did you talk with Mrs. Harrison during that shift?" Hal smoothed his mustache with his thumb and forefinger.

"Just in the break room around two. She was leaving as I was coming in, and we said hello. That was it." He shrugged his shoulders.

"Did she seem upset?"

Jim, apparently bored with the conversation to this point, shifted in his seat. "Did she mention leaving town?"

Michael looked at Hal. "No, she seemed fine." He turned to Jim. "She didn't mention going out of town to me."

"Thank you." Hal rose and followed Michael to the door. Hal and Jim endured the ensuing six interviews that all amounted to what they already knew. Elizabeth Harrison had seemed fine on Tuesday, had not mentioned leaving town to any of her coworkers, and had apparently left work alone.

         *   *   *

"What time is it?" Jim asked with a yawn.

Hal took his hand from the wheel and looked at his watch. "A little before three."

"So we just wasted about, what, two and a half hours?"

"I wouldn't say it was all wasted." Hal took a long drag from his cigarette. "We know her car wasn't in the Silver Peak parking lot before eleven p.m. on Tuesday."

"Yeah, we also know that nobody knows nothin' at that place. Whadda bunch of ass-kissin' morons!" Jim had obviously not taken kindly to the staff of the Silver Peak Hotel in Park City. "Did that kid seem jumpy to you?"

"Kimball?"

"Yeah. He was even startin' to make me nervous." Jim rolled a Lifesaver around in his mouth, clicking it with his teeth.

"Do you have to do that?" Hal was annoyed.

"Do you have to smoke?" Jim retorted.

Hal watched the road. The subject was apparently closed. "I'll run a background and records check on everyone we've talked to."

"Think we'll be working late tonight?"

"Probably. Why?"

Jim watched an attractive young brunette drive by in a blue Nissan. "They get younger every day." He turned to Hal as if he had just remembered the question. "I didn't set my VCR, and I was wonderin' if I'd have a chance to before the game started. Should be a good one."

"You could probably slip out for a while." Hal began going over the limited information they had come up with. He tried to piece together a theory or, at this point, merely a guess as to what had happened to Elizabeth Harrison. He was anxious to search Elizabeth's home. Perhaps it would yield some clue as to how she spent her last hours and who ultimately took her life. His instincts were telling him that the killer was not her husband, but possibly an easily-angered, jealous man with whom Elizabeth might be having an affair. Or maybe she desperately wanted to wound her husband's ego and planned a spur of the moment tryst with someone she hardly knew.

". . . don't you think?" Jim's round face was skewed into a look of puzzlement.

Hal had lost himself in thought and missed Jim's remarks. "What?"

"Geeze! Where are ya, buddy? Hello!" Jim seemed more amused by Hal's inattention than angered by it.

"I'm sorry," Hal apologized. "What were you saying?"

"You're somethin', you know that? Here I am, spillin' my guts, finally opening up to the one person I thought I could count on, and you missed every word." Jim shook his head in mock disappointment.

"Yeah, right."

"I was just saying that I think Perry getting that promotion stinks. Jarvis acts like Perry's the only guy that's ever done anything special." Jim's tone emphasized his resentment. "Any one of us woulda done the same thing. He just happened to be in the right place at the right time." He shook his head. "He's nothin' special."

Hal feigned indifference. "I've given up worryin' about who's going where in the department." Hal hoped his partner would not call him on his flagrant lie.

As they pulled into the station's parking garage, Hal assigned Jim the task of putting together a team to conduct a search of the Harrison's home and gather the necessary warrants and paperwork. Hal hustled from the car to his desk, not wanting to waste any time. He opened his notebook and looked up Helen Connor's phone number. After dialing, he browsed through the phone messages that sat on his desk and waited for an answer.

"Hello?" A man answered on the fourth ring.

"May I speak with Mrs. Connor, please?"

"Who's calling?" The man's voice was insistent.

"This is Sergeant Lund, with the Salt Lake Police Department. It's regarding her daughter." Hal tucked two messages from his wife into his shirt pocket.

"Just a minute."

There was a long silence before Helen Connor spoke. "Yes?"

"Mrs. Connor, I know this is a difficult time, but there are a few questions I need to ask you." Hal waited for a reply. "Ma'am?"

"Yes, I'm sorry." Helen sounded upset.

"What time did Elizabeth call you on Tuesday to have you pick your grandson up from the sitter?"

"Oh, I don't know. It was afternoon. Two or three."

"Okay. And what is the name and address of the sitter your daughter used?"

"It's the Little Willow Daycare Center on State Street just past Forty-fifth."

Hal wrote the information down. "Now, were there any friends or relatives that your daughter spent a lot of time with?"

"Not that I know of. She didn't have any brothers or sisters. I don't think she was close to any of her cousins. Her friends," Helen sighed, "I really don't know any of her friends."

"Thank you, Mrs. Connor. Again, I'm sorry to have bothered you at this time."

"Detective?"

"Yes?"

"Are you going to arrest my son-in-law?"

"We're still investigating the leads we have, and at this time we're not ready to make any arrests."

"He's guilty, you know. He killed Liz, and now he has my grandson." Helen's voice was filled with animosity.

Hal was unsure how to handle the conversation. "Do you really think he's responsible for your daughter's death?"

"Oh, there's no doubt. I don't trust him. I never have. Liz was trying to get away from him." She stressed the point. "Now he's come and taken Ryan. He was here with some people from the state. I can't believe they're making me turn my grandson over to a killer."

"We're doing everything we can, Mrs. Connor. We just . . ."

"If you were doing everything you could, Ryan would be safe with me."

"I'm sorry, ma'am, but we have no control over custody matters."

"I just want Craig where he belongs, and you're the only ones that can put him there. I have to go now, Detective." Helen's voice was cold.

"Thank you, Mrs. Connor. I'll be in . . ." Hal's sentence was cut short by the dial tone. He hung up and looked through his notes for Craig Harrison's phone number.

"Here's the information you wanted." Hal glanced up to find Warren Ellsworth standing before him. "Not much to go on."

Hal took the papers from Warren and looked over them. Listed were several homicides that were similar to Elizabeth Harrison's. "All but one of these guys are still in prison."

"Yeah. Do you want me to check the other one out?"

Hal thought for a second before answering. "Yeah. It's a long shot, but I want every possible lead followed up on." The officer started to walk away from Hal's desk. "Do you know if the coroner's report has come up yet?"

Warren turned around. "Haven't heard anything."

"Thanks." Hal picked up the phone and dialed Craig Harrison's phone number. Before it rang, he hung up. He wondered if Helen Connor were grasping at straws. It was possible she just disliked her son-in-law and would believe anything bad about him. Or, Craig Harrison could be capable of murdering his wife. He decided to contact him in person.

Jim walked out of Lieutenant Bonner's office and called out to Hal. "Coroner's report's on the way up."

"You got everything we need?" Hal stood up and walked toward Jim.

"Yeah. We're ready when you are."

"Who've we got for a crew?"

"Peterson, Ellsworth, Bartholomew and Jeffers."

Hal smiled, pleased with Jim's answer. "Good. Who've we got from the lab?"

"Roselli," Jim said in a singsong manner. He raised his eyebrows and donned a mischievous grin.

Hal was not amused by Jim's chauvinistic sarcasm. "She's good."

A young officer approached Hal and Jim. "Here's your report." He handed Hal a red folder.

"Thanks, Russ." Hal opened the folder and began reading. Jim unwrapped a piece of Juicy Fruit gum and shoved it in his mouth. Lieutenant Bonner got up from his desk and stood in the doorway of his office anticipating Hal's findings.

Hal looked up at the two men. "The autopsy shows that death most likely occurred between five and ten p.m. on Tuesday. If that's correct, she's not the one who parked her car at the hotel in Park City." Hal resumed reading.

"Do they give us any idea on the weapon?" Jim glanced over Hal's shoulder at the report.

Hal read from the report. "It says 'Cause of death was blunt force to the back of the skull causing massive brain trauma. Metal fragments found in the lesions, along with the size and consistency of the wounds, indicate a heavy steel object, cylindrical in shape, approximately one and one-half inches in diameter was used to inflict the injuries.'"

"Get me a copy of that, would ya?" Bonner asked as he returned to his desk.

"Yeah." Hal took an empty accordion file from his desk drawer and placed the coroner's report inside. He turned to Jim. "Let's go."

CHAPTER 6

"That's all I'm gonna get?" The woman sat with her jaw dropped in disbelief, staring at Jeni.

"Your husband is entitled to support himself." Jeni had a hard time biting her tongue.

"Oh, so he sleeps around on me, and I'm the one who pays!" The woman shifted in her seat. "I'm paying you to represent me, not him!" Her anger was rising with every word.

Jeni took a deep breath. "Mrs. Bird, I am representing you. The point I'm trying to make is that I cannot reasonably ask for a more lucrative settlement on your behalf." She paused. "We're asking for the home, one of the family cars, maximum child support, seventy percent of all other marital assets and an adequate alimony. Your husband will . . ."

"Adequate? You know, I'm going to have to get a job now to support me and the kids. I haven't worked in seventeen years!"

"Mrs. Bird, I know this is an extremely difficult situation, and I realize you are experiencing a great deal of anguish over this, but I encourage you to try and

refrain from letting your emotions override your reason."
Jeni was growing tired of the conversation.

She glanced at the time. It was ten minutes after
four. Mrs. Bird had now taken up ten minutes of Mr.
and Mrs. Jacobsen's time.

"Oooh, this is great, just great. I pay you lawyer fees
and get a shrink!" The woman stood up and gathered
her coat and purse. She gave Jeni a glaring look as she
rose from her chair. "What time is court?"

Jeni looked down at the paper on her desk. "Nine
a.m. It's in courtroom two on the third floor."

The woman muttered a reply.

"I'll be in the courtroom ten or fifteen minutes
early." Jeni smiled. Her gesture was not returned.

The woman walked out, and Jeni fell back into her
chair with a sigh. She allowed herself only a few seconds
respite. She stood, smoothed her burgundy skirt, and
gathered Mrs. Bird's file. As she exited her office, she
smiled at the couple who looked up in anticipation. She
handed the file to Kate and took the Jacobsen's file in
exchange.

"Jeni, this phone message came a few minutes ago."
Kate handed the message to Jeni.

Jeni read the message quickly, then turned to the
Jacobsens. "I apologize. I know I'm running a little late
already, but I'll need a minute to make this phone call."

"No problem." The man smiled and sat back on the
couch.

Jeni returned to her desk and called Craig Harrison.
"Mr. Harrison, this is Jenifer Sullivan."

"Oh, thank you for calling."

"How did it go with Mrs. Giles?" Jeni was anxious to know.

"Well, my mother-in-law wasn't going to cooperate with us, but Barbara explained that she would be in violation of the law. She gave Ryan to me, but not without a scene. I appreciate your help."

"I'm glad things worked out."

"Well, another situation has come up that I could use your advice on." Craig sounded almost timid.

"Yes?"

"The detective that is investigating my wife's death came by my apartment about twenty minutes ago. He told me they were on their way to search our house." Craig paused. "They want to talk with me in a couple of hours, and they strongly suggested I have an attorney with me."

Jeni thought for a moment before asking, "Do they consider you a suspect?"

"I'm afraid so. What do you suggest I do?"

"When and where will they be questioning you?"

"They asked me if I would mind going to the station. They stressed the point that I didn't have to, but I don't see why I shouldn't. They're expecting me there at six-thirty."

Jeni's mind went over the situation. Was she prepared to take it on, or should she recommend a criminal defense attorney? "Are you asking for my opinion, or my representation?"

"Do you think I should have an attorney?"

"I think whenever you're dealing with a matter of this magnitude and importance, it's wise to have counsel of some type."

"Can I hire you?" The conversation seemed very awkward for Craig.

"Yes. I'll represent you." She sounded assured with her answer, but inside doubts were still echoing.

"Thank you."

"Could you come to my office around six? We can discuss things and go from here."

"Yes, that's fine. I really appreciate your help." Craig sounded relieved.

"I'll see you at six." Jeni hung up, feeling a little insecure in her decision. She was unsure of what she was getting herself involved in.

"Sorry to keep you waiting." Jeni held the door as Mr. and Mrs. Jacobsen entered her office. She showed the couple to a comfortable sofa and sat in the chair beside it. "I have good news. The father signed the papers Friday."

"Yes!" Mr. Jacobsen grabbed his wife's hand and gave it a squeeze.

"Does this mean it's final?" Mrs. Jacobsen was reluctant to celebrate without knowing.

"It will be as soon as I can get you before a judge." Jeni beamed.

"Oh, thank God!" Mrs. Jacobsen's eyes welled up with tears. "We've waited so long!" Her husband put his arms around her shoulders. "She's finally ours. Honey, she's ours!"

Jeni allowed them a moment before continuing. "He does want to be able to have some contact with her but will not insist that she know he is her father."

Mr. Jacobsen looked at his wife. "We can live with that." His wife nodded in agreement.

"I've called the court clerk, and she'll be calling me back in the morning to give me a court time. I'm guessing that it will be Thursday or Friday."

"Okay." Mr. Jacobsen sat on the edge of the couch and looked as though he could hardly contain his elation.

"I need you to go over these papers before I file them, to make sure everything is in order." Jeni opened the file and handed the papers to Mrs. Jacobsen. "I'll give you a minute to read through those." She was moved by the joy she saw in her clients' faces. It was at times like this that she most loved her job.

*   *   *

"If there's nothing else, I'll be going." Kate stood in the doorway.

It took Jeni a moment to focus on Kate and comprehend what she had said. "Oh, no, I don't need anything else. Thanks for staying late."

"Sure." Kate lingered in the doorway, looking at Jeni as though she had something to add.

"Have a good night." Jeni watched Kate walk out, then went back to reading.

Kate got to the outer door of the office and turned back. "Jeni, you really need to slow down a little. I'm afraid you're going to burn yourself out."

Jeni smiled at Kate's well-meant advice. "Thanks, Kate. I'm doing all right."

"I just worry about you."

"I know, but I really am fine."

"See you tomorrow." With that she was gone.

Jeni had twenty-five minutes to prepare for her meeting with Craig Harrison. She had to be ready to make a decision as to whether or not she would represent him if he were formally charged with his wife's murder. Her prosecution of countless criminals involved offenses running the gamut of crime, but Jeni had never prosecuted a murder case. Was she prepared to act as a defense attorney in one?

Premature thinking, she thought. He might not even be a suspect. On the other hand, he could be the culprit. She began a debate within herself as to his possible guilt or innocence. He seemed like a very nice man, calm and polite. Yet, if nothing else, Jeni's experience as a trial lawyer had taught her that things were not always as they appeared. The Harrisons were going through a divorce. It seemed to be benign, but passion and the heat of anger could turn simple arguments into deadly fights, she thought. "No," she said aloud.

Jeni opened her book and took up reading where she had left off, the chapter on criminal interrogation.

CHAPTER 7

The sun filtered down through thin layers of soft, white clouds and caught Harold Lund's eye as he stepped onto Elizabeth Harrison's redwood deck. Behind him, several officers were carefully sifting through the items inside the home, searching for evidence.

Hal scanned the backyard, not really knowing what he was looking for. A sandbox in the corner of the yard was filled with toys, pails and a few plastic shovels. In the middle of the lawn was a sturdy swing set.

"Lund, we've got a woman out here that says she's a relative of Mrs. Harrison's. She wants to know about a cat." A hulking man in a tight blue police uniform approached Hal on the deck.

"I'll be right out." Hal walked through the sliding glass doors that led to the family room and looked for Jim. "Have you seen Webber?" he asked Warren Ellsworth.

"He's down the hall."

Hal went to the hallway and called out to Jim. "Jim, I need you outside for a minute."

Jim poked his head out of the room at the end of the hall. "Okay. Just a sec." A moment later he emerged to join Hal. "What's up?"

"A woman outside who says she's a relative." Hal spoke as they approached the side door of the house. As they stepped out onto the small cement porch, they saw two uniformed officers talking with a tall, slender woman who was visibly upset. The woman looked at Hal as he and Jim approached. Hal thought she looked vaguely familiar.

"Ma'am, I'm Sergeant Lund, Salt Lake PD. You say you're a relative of Mrs. Harrison's?"

The woman pulled her arm from the grip of a tall officer. "I'm Liz's sister-in-law, Danielle Harrison. I came by to get Sammy, her cat, and pick up a few things of Ryan's." She tried hard to choke back the sobs that were forming, but they were too powerful.

Hal nodded to the officers and motioned for them to back off. The woman buried her face in her hands for a moment before regaining her composure. As she wiped the tears from her deep brown eyes, Hal realized why she had looked familiar. Her eyes were very much like her brother Craig's, as was her short, neatly kept black hair.

"I'm very sorry about your sister-in-law." Hal offered his condolences. "Would you mind answering a few questions for us?"

"What about the cat? Is the cat all right?" The tears refused to stop flowing.

"The cat's fine, Ms. Harrison. We called animal control to come and pick it up, but they haven't arrived yet. I see no harm in letting you take it." Hal smoothed his mustache. "As for taking any other items out of the house, I'm afraid you won't be able to, yet."

The woman looked at Hal. Her eyes were filled with desperation. "Could you please tell me what happened to her?"

"Ms. Harrison, we're trying to piece together the information we have, to determine just that. Maybe you could help us." Hal took a pen and a small notebook from his jacket pocket. "When was the last time you saw Elizabeth?"

"I've been in Chicago on business since the nineteenth. I got back Sunday morning. I saw Liz the day before I left." Danielle's voice was strained with emotion.

Hal noticed a gathering of people moving closer and let Danielle behind the police barrier, onto the porch. "Were you close to your sister-in-law?"

"She was more than my brother's wife; she was my friend. We've been friends since the second grade." Danielle put her clenched hand up to her lips. "Yes, we were close."

"Do you know of anyone who held bad feelings for Elizabeth or might have wanted to harm her?" Hal handed the notebook and pen to Jim, who began taking notes.

"No." She seemed surprised by the question.

"Did Elizabeth and your brother ever fight?" Hal's questions were becoming more direct.

"They had their disagreements, but they never fought." She emphasized her last words.

"How was your brother handling their divorce?"

Danielle hesitated. "You'd have to ask my brother."

"Does your brother have a hot temper, fly off the handle easily?"

Danielle's eyes grew angry as she realized what Hal was implicating. "No. Craig is very easygoing. He would never hurt anyone."

"Was Elizabeth involved with anyone else?"

"Involved? You mean was Liz having an affair?" Danielle spoke with an almost indignant tone.

Hal just looked at Danielle without answering.

"No. No, she wasn't involved with anyone. Look, I would just like to get the cat and take him home. I'd be happy to answer your questions when I feel a little more stable."

"Jim, could you get the cat for her?" He watched as Jim rolled his eyes and went into the house. "Thank you for your help, Ms. Harrison. I'm sorry to have upset you. Here is my card." Hal took a card from his pocket and offered it to Danielle. "Please call me if you have any information you feel might help us."

"I will." Danielle put the card in the back pocket of her Levi's. "When will I be able to get Ryan's things?"

"We should be able to let you in tomorrow, if that would be all right."

Jim walked out of the house, carrying an orange and white cat at arm's length. "Here ya go."

*   *   *

Hal Lund was the last one into the conference room. He shut the door and took a seat next to Merril Bonner. "Okay, let's go over what we've got." He opened the file he had brought with him. Leon Peterson, Warren Ellsworth, Blake Bartholomew, Ron Jeffers, Jim Webber and Lieutenant Bonner all looked to Hal in expectation.

"First, what we know, and I'll tell you it's not very much at this point." Hal pulled out the coroner's report. "Elizabeth Harrison was killed on September twenty-first. Looks like sometime between five and ten p.m. The victim was struck five times in the back of the head with a heavy steel bar, possibly a crowbar or something similar." Hal retrieved four photos of Elizabeth's battered skull and tossed them onto the middle of the table.

"The murder weapon hasn't been found, correct?" Blake Bartholomew looked up from the notes he was taking and waited for Hal's response.

"Right. We are obtaining search warrants for other possibilities." Hal flipped the pages of the report. "We also know that she was not killed where her body was found. There were no blood spatters, no sign of a struggle. There were dirt particles and sawdust found on her clothing that were inconsistent with the soil where we found her. Also, the postmortem bruises found on her arms, legs and back were presumably inflicted by moving the body. Traces of carbon monoxide were found on her skin, indicating that her body was transported in a vehicle."

"Hers?" Leon Peterson questioned.

"No. There were no traces of blood in her car.
From the lab analysis we can assume that the victim was
not in her car during or after her murder." Hal took a
cigarette from his pocket and held it up. "Anyone
mind?"

The men around the table all shook their heads.
Jim rolled his eyes. "It's your seven minutes, pal."

Hal lit the cigarette and pulled an ashtray over from
across the table. "Okay, we also know that robbery
wasn't a motive. Her purse was found in her unlocked
car. It contained sixty-seven dollars in cash, her checkbook and several credit cards. Her wedding ring was
still on her finger." Hal took a drag from his Winston.
"We can assume that this was not a random act of
violence. The victim was not sexually assaulted, and as
I said, her personal belongings were not taken. There is
one thing that's really bugging the hell out of me." Hal
paused as if to increase suspense. "Her car. We have a
security guard that swears her vehicle was not in the
Silver Peak parking lot before he got off duty at eleven
p.m. on the night she was killed. Elizabeth Harrison was
five foot seven. The driver's seat of her car was moved
as far back as it will go. She wouldn't have been able to
reach the pedals in the position it was in. From this, we
can assume that her car was placed there by someone
else after her death and possibly after her body was
dumped up Emigration Canyon."

"What have we got in the way of suspects?" Merril Bonner looked over at Hal.

"Well, traces of what they believe is a men's cologne were found on the victim's clothing. That, the force of the blows, and the fact that her body was obviously carried lead us to assume it was a man."

"I don't know. I ran into a woman at the grocery store the other day—she smelled like Elsha and coulda kicked my ass." A mischievous grin slithered across Jim's face.

"My nine-year-old daughter could kick your ass," Ron Jeffers interjected with a chuckle.

Hal, unamused with their banter, continued, "The victim and her husband were going through a divorce. According to the victim's mother, they had been fighting the night before she was killed. So, we have to consider him a suspect. We have a jumpy kid that works at the Silver Peak, where her car was found, who has a criminal record for assault. In fact, he's on probation for assaulting a former girlfriend," Hal paused, "with a hammer."

"Very interesting," Ron Jeffers spoke up. "What's his name?"

"Jeremy Kimball. We've got a file on him right here." Hal shuffled through his papers and found the information on Kimball.

"He seemed pretty nervous this afternoon when we spoke to him," Jim added.

"He worked until six p.m. the night Mrs. Harrison was killed. He says he went to Albertson's for a few groceries after leaving work, then spent the night in his apartment watching videos."

"So they're the only suspects we have so far?" Bonner questioned Hal.

"Right now they're all we've got."

"What does your gut tell ya?"

Hal turned to his lieutenant. "My gut tells me we don't have the whole story yet. I think it's possible she was having an affair or looking for a one-night stand. I'm not ready to point my finger at someone in court and say he did it. Not yet."

"Anything else?" Bonner leaned forward.

"Well, we've got a few footprints from where the body was found. We've got the lab working on them. All we know right now is that it appears to be some type of men's boot, size nine and a half or ten." Hal put his cigarette out. "We also have a button. Roselli is running tests on the threads to see what type of fabric it was on. A lot of the coroner's report isn't in yet, and the lab's working on some things. That's about it." Hal began gathering the papers and photographs he had strewn across the table. He rose and tucked them into the file folder. "We're questioning the husband," Hal looked down at his watch. "He should be here at six-thirty."

Merril Bonner rose and stood next to Hal. "Who do you want in there with you?"

Hal had assumed his lieutenant would make that decision and was pleasantly surprised that he had asked for Hal's view. "Jim and Leon." Hal had great respect for Leon Peterson's experience and interrogation techniques. "Let's have the others monitor from outside."

Bonner nodded in compliance and followed Hal from the conference room. As the group of men started down the hall, Merril Bonner put a halting hand on Hal's shoulder. "Be careful with this one." The statement was probably not intended to wound; nevertheless, it struck a blow to Hal's confidence.

CHAPTER 8

"Sorry I'm late." Craig Harrison offered an apology as he entered Jeni's office.

Jeni glanced at her clock. It was three minutes after six. "You're fine. Please, have a seat."

Craig sat down with a heavy sigh. "Do you have any idea what sort of things they're going to ask me?" His anxiety was evident.

"Well, if they are considering you a suspect, they'll probably . . ."

"They are. I just dropped Ryan off at my sister's. When we found out they were going to search the house, she went down to get Liz's cat and some of Ryan's things. They questioned her about me and Liz. She got the impression that they think I—they think I killed her."

Jeni sat silently for a moment before speaking. "They will ask you questions about your relationship, your feelings toward your wife. They'll delve as deeply as you let them into your personal life. What you need to remember is that you're in control. Tell them only what you feel comfortable in telling them." Jeni looked at the forlorn man who sat across from her. "They may badger you, try to rile you. They might even try to get you to incriminate yourself. Don't fall into any traps."

Craig looked confused. "What do you mean, traps?"

Jeni rose from her chair and slowly walked around to the front of her desk. "Mr. Harrison, do you love your son?"

The question seemed to add to Craig's confusion. "Of course I do."

"Would you go to great lengths for him?"

"Yes." Craig appeared apprehensive.

"Your son was living with your wife, correct?" Jeni's face was expressionless.

"Yes."

"Your son will be living with you now?"

"Yes."

"I'm sure that will be a major adjustment in your life." Jeni smiled.

"Not really. I've only been living alone for a month now."

"So, you're pleased that your son is with you."

Craig seemed to be relaxing. "Oh, yeah! I never wanted to move away from him. It was . . ."

Jeni interrupted. "So, your wife's death leaves you with uncontested custody." Jeni walked over and sat in a chair next to Craig. "That's what I mean by traps. When they ask you a question, be honest and be succinct. Like I said, you are in control of this interview. Don't give that control over to them."

Craig's face was pained. "What if I say something stupid, or an answer just doesn't come out right?"

"I'll be right there. Look over at me, and if I nod, go ahead and answer. Otherwise, I'll intercede. I won't let them intimidate you."

Craig stared down at the carpet as though searching the threads for a resolution to his bewilderment. "How can everything change so fast?" He shook his head. "One day you're with your wife and son—everything's great—six months later your wife's dead, and the finger's pointed at you. Everything just fell apart. Why couldn't she have . . ." His last words were cut short by emotion.

Jeni felt a twinge deep in her chest as she witnessed this brawny, muscular man transform into a defenseless child. His breathing became erratic as he tried to repress the sobs that were heaving his chest. She rose and draped her arm over his shoulders in an attempt to comfort. She felt powerless.

*   *   *

The front desk at the Salt Lake City Police Station was swarming with people. Two uniformed officers were restraining a handcuffed man who had attempted to climb over the counter in search of a phone. "I want my call, you fuckin' pigs!" he yelled repeatedly. A Hispanic woman in obvious distress frantically explained her situation in rapid Spanish to a female officer. People were coming and going in haste, much like at a fast-food restaurant during lunch hour.

Craig Harrison sat quietly, watching the commotion with little expression. He looked down at his watch and shifted nervously in his seat.

"Are you all right?" Jenifer Sullivan asked her client with concern.

"Yeah. Just a little nervous."

"Mr. Harrison." Craig and Jeni looked up at Harold Lund. "If you'll come with us."

Craig stood. "Yes."

Jeni rose and introduced herself to Hal. "My name is Jenifer Sullivan. I'm Mr. Harrison's attorney."

Hal could not help but smile. He nodded at Jeni and wondered if the young woman had any idea what he was thinking. She looked too young and was far too pretty to be a lawyer. Although, with legs like that, she could definitely make an impression in a courtroom, or anywhere else, for that matter.

"Hal?" Jim stuck an elbow into his distracted partner's ribs.

"If you'll come with us, please." Hal gestured toward the double doors that led to the detective division.

Jeni looked over at Craig as they walked down the corridor. His eyes were wide, much like the eyes of an animal mesmerized by car headlights racing toward it. She watched the blood drain from his face as cold beads of sweat formed on his upper lip.

Hal stopped halfway down the hall and opened the door to a small room. "Please, take a seat and we'll be right with you." Craig followed Jeni into the room. "Would you care for anything to drink? Coffee, soda, juice?" Hal stood in the doorway.

Craig shook his head, unable to speak. Jeni noticed two carafes filled with icewater and a stack of paper cups on the table. "No, thank you," she answered with a smile. "We'll be right back." Hal and Jim closed the door, leaving Jeni alone with her client. She looked over at Craig, who sat next to her on one side of a large table. His hands were clenched, his knuckles white.

"Relax. You'll be all right." Jeni reassured Craig. "Just take a deep breath."

Craig tried to speak, but could not find his voice. He cleared his throat and swallowed hard. "It's just starting to sink in, what they're accusing me of."

"You haven't been accused of anything yet." Jeni was nervous herself and hoped she was masking it well.

The door opened, and both Craig and Jeni looked up to see three men walk in and sit down across the table from them. Hal looked at Craig, then turned to Jeni. "I'm Sergeant Lund. This is Detective Webber," he gestured at Jim, "and this is Sergeant Peterson." Hal motioned toward Leon Peterson, who nodded with a smile.

"Gentlemen," Jeni acknowledged. She took a notebook and pen from her briefcase and placed them before her on the table.

"Mr. Harrison, we would like your permission to record this interview." Hal pushed a tape recorder into the middle of the table.

Craig looked to Jeni before answering. Jeni nodded. "Okay." Craig's voice was shaky.

Hal pushed the record button on the tape recorder. After stating the date and time, and naming the individuals present, Hal paused and looked at Craig. "Mr. Harrison, as you know, we are investigating your wife's murder. We are obligated to tell you, before beginning this interview, that you are being considered a suspect." Craig flinched. Hal continued, "You have the privilege at any time during this proceeding to refuse to answer any question or provide any evidence that may result in self-incrimination. Any information provided by this interview may be used against you if any charges are subsequently filed against you. Do you understand these privileges, Mr. Harrison?"

Craig looked to Jeni, then nodded in understanding. "Yes."

"Now, Mr. Harrison, you and your wife were separated, correct?" Hal looked intently at Craig.

"Yes."

"How long had you been separated?"

"I, uh, moved into my own apartment August fifteenth. So, a little over a month." Craig looked for Jeni's approval and received a nod.

"Had you or your wife filed for divorce?" Hal continued his questions.

"No. We were about to." Craig noticed Jim taking notes. Jim looked up after jotting down Craig's reply, then he continued writing. Craig's anxiety seemed to escalate.

"Was your relationship with your wife hostile?"

Craig looked back to Hal. "No."

"Mr. Harrison, we have sources that will testify that you were arguing with your wife the night before she was killed." Hal leaned forward and rested his chin in his hand.

"I . . ."

Jeni interrupted Craig's answer. "Sergeant Lund, unless you are prepared to name those sources and produce their statements, I suggest that you not bring their assertions into this interrogation."

Hal clenched his jaw and shot a glance at Jeni. "Mr. Harrison, were you and your wife arguing the night before she died?"

"No." Craig poured himself a glass of water.

Hal pulled a cassette tape from a large envelope that lay before him on the table. He held it up, his eyes narrowing at Craig. "This tape is from your wife's answering machine. We'd like you to listen to this message." Hal handed the tape to Leon Peterson. Leon placed it in a small cassette player and pushed play. The room was silent as they all listened for the message.

"Hi," hearing his own voice, Craig put a hand to his forehead and began massaging it. "I just wanted to apologize for last night. I guess I'll talk to you after work. Bye."

Leon stopped the tape. Hal leaned back in his chair with a smug look. "Was that your voice, Mr. Harrison?"

Craig looked as though he was becoming physically ill. "Yes," he answered.

"Were you apologizing for an argument?"

Craig looked at Hal, then turned to Jeni. Jeni's eyes concentrated on Craig's, as though trying to send a telepathic message. "No." Craig looked down at the table.

Hal resumed. "What were you apologizing for?"

Jeni intercepted the question. "My client has indicated that he and his wife were not arguing." She looked to Craig and shook her head. "He does not need to further clarify that fact."

Hal took a deep breath. "When was the last time you saw your wife?"

Craig swallowed a cold sip of water. "Last Monday."

Seeing that Craig was not going to elaborate on his answer, Hal prodded him. "And what were the circumstances?"

Craig looked to Jeni. Jeni signaled for Craig to answer. "I took her and Ryan out to dinner."

"Did you have a disagreement?"

"No. I was going to fix the leak in the washroom after dinner, but I was called out to a job site to look over a problem. That's why I called the next morning to apologize." Craig's face became flushed.

Hal looked at Craig for a long moment before continuing. "Were you or your wife having an affair?"

"No." Craig was quick to reply.

Hal put a clenched fist to his mouth and cleared his throat. His fingers pressed his mustache to his upper lip as he contemplated his next question. "Do you know of anyone who harbored bad feelings toward you or your wife? Anyone who would want to harm either one of you?"

"No."

Hal turned to Leon Peterson and nodded. Receiving this signal from Hal, Leon took up the reins. "Mr. Harrison, you own your own construction company?"

"Yes."

"Did your wife own interest in this company?"

Craig looked to Jeni for coaching. Seeing Craig's distress, Jeni turned to Leon. "I was handling the Harrisons' divorce. Mrs. Harrison was involved in the initial loan for the business. That loan has been paid off, and Mrs. Harrison's name is in no way involved with the company."

Leon narrowed his eyes as he spoke to Jeni. "I trust that when we investigate the paperwork we will find that to be true?"

"Yes, Sergeant." Jeni was trying not to be offended by the officer's attitude.

Leon turned his attention back to Craig. "Was your wife covered by life insurance?"

"Yes." Craig took a long drink from his cup.

"Who was the primary beneficiary of that policy, Mr. Harrison?" Leon Peterson's eyes concentrated on Craig.

"Me and Ryan, our son." Craig put a hand to his head as if to stop it from spinning.

"Do you know the amount of the policy?"

Craig was distracted by Hal whispering something to Jim Webber.

"Mr. Harrison?" Leon prodded Craig.

He shook his head slowly. "No, I'm not sure." His voice was almost nonexistent.

"Where were you last Tuesday between five and eleven p.m.?"

Craig's face expressed panic as he appeared to search his memory for the answer. "I was in Vernal Tuesday. I got home around ten-thirty."

"What were you doing in Vernal?" Leon asked.

"I—I was there on business." Craig brought a hand up to rub the back of his neck.

"Were you with someone or alone?" Leon's eyes remained locked on Craig's face as he carefully registered his reactions to each question.

"I was alone." Moisture formed on Craig's upper lip and his face grew pale.

"On the phone message you left," Leon pointed to the recorder on the table, "you said you'd talk to her after work on Tuesday. Did you intend on seeing her?"

"Yes—I mean yes, I intended to talk to her, but when I called she wasn't home."

"But you didn't leave another message," Leon pointed out.

"No. It was late, so I—I didn't leave a message." Craig looked to Jeni with frightened eyes.

"Gentlemen, I'm sure you all have, at one time or another, called someone whom you find is not at home, but you decide not to leave a message." Jeni smiled. Her smile dimmed over the next two hours as the three detectives continued to grill Jeni's client about his failing marriage and his whereabouts the night his wife was killed.

*   *   *

Craig and Jeni walked silently toward the front desk of the Salt Lake City Police Station. As the glass door leading outside came into view, Craig's pace quickened. He rushed toward the door as if relief from his pain and trepidation waited just outside of it. He pushed open the door as if blocking for a running back. Stopping and looking up, he seemed surprised by the cold drops of rain that greeted him.

They had been cooped up in that small, windowless interrogation room for over two hours. Dusk was quickly turning to night, and heavy, gray clouds shrouded the stars and dusted the ground with droplets of water. Craig took in a deep breath, as if he had just surfaced from a bottomless pool.

"Guess we shouldn't have walked, huh?" Jeni held her briefcase above her to shield the rain.

The raindrops that fell on Craig's cheeks did little to camouflage the moisture forming in his eyes. He took several more deep breaths and turned to Jeni. "What do I do now?"

Jeni was at a loss for words. She looked at this man with whom she had just become acquainted and felt as though their lives were now irreversibly intertwined. She had developed the ability to separate her life from those of her clients and to remain emotionally uninvolved, but Craig Harrison was challenging those abilities. She looked into his dark brown eyes, swimming in fear and frustration. She could not help but ache at the signs of pain in his face, and she could not help but feel guilty at finding him so attractive.

"Would you like to stop for a cup of coffee? There's a coffeehouse just down the street. It's on the way to my office." Jeni waited for a reply.

"Sure." Craig was regaining his composure.

The smell of wet asphalt and fresh rain made the chill of their walk more bearable for Jeni. She was reminded of her childhood, when she and her brothers would ride their bikes in the street in front of their house, taking careful aim to hit the puddles, holding their feet up to avoid the splash. Her brothers still teased her about her attempts to save all the worms that the rain brought out from the sun's deadly rays. As soon as the rain stopped, she would run out to the driveway and pick up worms, tossing them back into the flower beds. The memory made her smile.

"You know, I haven't even asked how much you charge." Craig's voice brought Jeni back from her reverie. "I'm not really sure I can afford you if this gets any worse."

"I'm flexible. We'll come up with something that works for both of us." Jeni spoke without looking at Craig from under her briefcase. They stopped in front of the coffee shop, and Craig opened the door for Jeni. They made their way to a table in the back and sat down.

"If you're hungry at all, they have wonderful sand-wiches." Jeni offered the recommendation as she opened a menu. A young waitress with an overabundance of energy took their orders and brought their coffee.

Craig stared into his mug as he stirred creamer into the rich, dark coffee. "I'm really scared." He looked across the table at Jeni. "I don't even know what to feel anymore. I know our marriage was a failure, but I really loved my wife, you know? I've lost my best friend." His voice cracked with emotion. He stared again into the caramel-colored substance in his mug. "I love my son more than anything, but I'm scared of raising him alone. And I'm even more afraid that I won't get that chance." He took a sip of his coffee. "They believe that I killed her. How can they think I'd kill her?"

It was a question Jeni could not answer. She could not answer her own question, which was how she could be so convinced that he had not killed her. But she was convinced. "We just need to find some way of proving that you were in Vernal last Tuesday evening when your wife was killed." She pushed her coffee into the middle of the table, so the waitress could put her sandwich in front of her. "Thank you."

The waitress placed Craig's sandwich on the table and left. Jeni watched her walk away, then reached out for Craig's hand which rested on the table. She gave it a gentle squeeze and released it. "I'll do everything I can to help you, including advising you against putting that honey on your pastrami on rye."

Craig looked at the bottle of honey he held over his sandwich. "I guess mustard would be better," he said with a smile, exposing two rows of perfect white teeth and a charming set of dimples. It was the first time Jeni had seen Craig smile. She had the feeling it was something she could easily get used to.

CHAPTER 9

Hal pulled into the driveway of his home and cringed when he saw the living room light still burning. He shut off the engine and sat for a moment, enjoying the last few drags of his Winston. Jean Lund peeked through a gap in the curtains and saw the glowing red end of her husband's cigarette. She sat back down on the couch and waited for his entrance. It seemed like an eternity, though it was only a few minutes before the front door opened.

"Hi, hun." Hal's greeting was dispassionate.

"Why didn't you call?" Jean tried not to sound upset.

Hal removed his suit jacket and rubbed his face with both hands. "You wouldn't believe the day I've had. I'm sorry, I should have called." He walked into the kitchen and returned with a bottle of Budweiser in his hand. He sat down in an armchair across the room from Jean. "This case is going to keep me pretty busy for the next little while."

Jean looked at the clock. It was almost eleven. She had not seen her husband since six-thirty that morning, and she did not know when she would have another opportunity to talk to him. It was now or never. "Hal, we need to talk."

Hal's eyes rolled, and he tossed his head back to take a gulp of his beer. "Jean, can't it wait? I have so much on my mind right now."

A tear formed and slowly made its way down Jean's cheek. "No, it can't wait." She brushed the tear from her face. "Do you know how long it's been since we've talked about anything?" Her question went unanswered. "We don't talk about your job, we don't talk about mine, we don't talk about us. What's happened?"

"What's happened is that I've been busy as hell." Hal drank down another portion of his beer.

"That's not it. You're different. You used to tell me what was going on in your life, how you felt about things. Ever since Trish left home you've become more distant. It's like the only thing that kept us together was the kids, and now that they've all moved out you don't want to stay." Jean struggled to control her emotions.

"That's bullshit!" Hal became defensive. It was true he was becoming more distant. He knew that. He did not know why he had started doubting his love for his wife, fantasizing about leaving her and wanting to run; but he did not think it had anything to do with their youngest daughter going off to college. "Let's go to bed." Hal rose and started to walk away.

"No! Don't shut me out, Hal. Not this time," Jean begged.

"What do you want from me?" Hal's voice intensified.

"I want my husband back." The tears began to flow freely now, and Jean reached for a tissue. "I want to know where I stand. I want to know you're there for me. I want to feel like I'm a part of your life again." Jean looked up at Hal. "What is it that you think I want?"

"I don't know anymore, Jeanie." Hal felt his chest heave as he let out this secret he had been keeping inside. "I don't know what I want anymore."

There was an almost unbearable silence. Jean took a deep breath. "I found a lump a few weeks ago. I went to . . ."

"A lump? What kind of a lump?" Hal's voice softened.

"A lump in my breast."

Hal slowly stepped backwards and sat back into the chair. "Why didn't you tell me?"

"I tried, Hal." Jean dabbed her eyes with the tissue. "I went to the doctor today. They did a sonagram and then a needle biopsy."

Hal thought of the two phone messages from Jean that he had left in his pocket, unanswered. He shook his head. "What did they say?"

"It doesn't look good. I have to go in for a biopsy a week from Wednesday. If they find it's cancer, they'll probably do a mastectomy right then and there."

"Oh my God." The news was something Hal had never expected. He sat for a moment, letting the repercussions of the impact subside. "Who's doing the surgery?" Hal stared blankly at the floor.

"Dr. Thomas."

"Good." Hal looked over at his wife, who sat on the edge of the couch, teetering like a frightened child. His heart stirred. In one brief moment Hal experienced a full range of emotion—guilt, anger, grief, compassion and fear. After the initial wave of panic receded, Hal fell back on the aptitude that made him a successful detective: following his instincts. His first impulse was to comfort his wife.

Hal moved to the couch and pulled Jean close to him. "It's all right, Jeanie," he whispered in her ear. "Everything's gonna be all right." They sat in silence, Jean's tears falling softly on Hal's shoulder.

*   *   *

Lack of sleep was catching up with Hal. It was just one more thing to remind him of the passing of his youth. He was on his third cup of coffee when Jim ambled in.

"Where's the funeral?" Jim polished off a glazed doughnut and waited for Hal to respond to his dig.

Hal looked up at the cumbersome man hovering over him. "I don't know, but if you go, wearing that tie, you're likely to be the one they bury."

"Who pissed in your Cheerios?" Jim feigned offense.

"Hey," Ron Jeffers called out as he approached Hal and Jim. "I hate to interrupt this little love spat, but I've got your search warrants." He handed a file to Hal.

"Thanks." Hal opened the folder and looked through the paperwork.

"Where do you want us?" Ron asked, referring to himself and his partner, Blake Bartholomew.

"We're waiting on a subpoena for Jeremy Kimball. When it gets here, we'll send you up to get him. That won't be until around nine."

"Okay." Ron started to walk away. "Nice tie, Jim!" he called over his shoulder.

"Jealousy rears its ugly head again." Jim smoothed his tie as he admired it. "Do ya think this Kimball guy had anything to do with it?"

"I'm not going to rule him out, but I have my doubts," Hal answered. "What do you think?"

"I think if he did it, he's not very smart." He shook his head and added, "Naw, the husband smells of guilt. He's the one I'm puttin' my money on."

"Well, as soon as Leon and Warren get here, we'll go see if we can prove your theory. We have warrants to search his apartment, his business office and his vehicles." Hal sipped his coffee. "Personally, I think we'll prove it wrong."

"Willing to put your money where your mouth is?"

Hal shook his head. "I can't believe you. I'm not about to start wagering on the guilt or innocence of our suspects. Stick to football, buddy."

"I woulda lost money last night." Jim's disgust was evident.

"Did you watch the game?"

"No. Hell, I was here 'til almost ten. I read about it in the paper. What time did you get outa here?"

"Ten-thirty, I think." Hal's mind went to his wife. For the first time in a long while, Hal had a hard time leaving her that morning. He thought of Jean, how childlike she had been in his arms, how secure he had felt holding her. Again, fear pierced his thoughts. He had considered leaving her, though never with conviction; but her leaving had never entered his mind. Now, everything seemed insignificant, even Elizabeth Harrison's murder, as he faced the possibility of losing his wife.

"Hello?" Jim interrupted Hal's reflection. "We're ready when you are."

Hal looked up to see Warren and Leon standing with Jim. He glanced at the clock. It was a few minutes after eight. "Okay, I'm ready."

CHAPTER 10

"Excuse me." A tall, dark-haired woman approached Jeni as she exited the courtroom.

"Yes?" The woman looked familiar, but Jeni couldn't place her.

"Are you Jenifer Sullivan?"

"Yes."

"I'm Danielle Harrison, Craig's sister."

"Oh, yes, I can see the resemblance." She offered her hand to Danielle. "It's a pleasure to meet you."

"Ms. Sullivan, I need your help." Her eyes were wide and beseeching.

Jeni could see the matter was serious. "Okay."

"Craig's just been arrested. I went to your office, and they told me I'd find you here."

Jeni was jolted by the news. "When did this happen?"

"About an hour ago. He called me from the jail."

Jeni was still reeling from the shock. "I can't believe they arrested him. What evidence could . . ."

Danielle interrupted her. "They found a tire iron in his truck that they think is the murder weapon." She broke into tears. "Craig wouldn't hurt anybody. He didn't kill Liz." Her words were choked by sobs.

Jeni offered a calming hand on her shoulder. "I'll do everything I can to help him."

Jeni instructed Danielle to wait for her at her office. The county jail was at the southeast corner of the court complex. Jeni exited the circuit court building and hurried down the steps. She checked her watch. Her next appointment was at one o'clock. That gave her a little over an hour.

*   *   *

The stench worsened with every step down the jail's corridor. It was unlike any odor Jeni had ever experienced: stale, rancid and lingering. Jeni felt as though she were visiting a place from another time. The walls were a dingy gray, the floor tiles old, chipped and fading. Though she had been instrumental in sending many individuals here, she had never been inside the jail herself. It was much different than she had imagined.

An attractive young woman with long, auburn hair led Jeni to the visiting area. "They'll be bringing him down in just a minute."

"Thanks." Jeni looked around the colorless room, which contained only a small table and two chairs. She could hear the echo of metal doors opening and closing, distant voices and footsteps. She felt an anxiety she could not rationalize, a fear she did not understand. Her uneasiness intensified as the steps grew closer.

Craig was escorted into the room in shackles and handcuffs. His face was pallid, his expression one of dismay. He was dressed in a bright orange jumpsuit, branded with bold black letters stating he was an inmate of the Salt Lake County Jail.

"You want these left on?" The officer motioned to Craig's handcuffs.

"No," Jeni replied.

The officer removed the restraints from Craig's wrists and ankles. "We'll be right outside the door," he said in a slow southern drawl. "If you need anything, knock."

The door shut with a loud report. Jeni could see the two guards through a window the size of a small picture frame in the door. She wondered if she were being foolish, having no fear of this man she hardly knew.

"What happened?" Jeni's voice was compassionate.

Staring at the table, Craig shook his head. It was a moment before he spoke. "They came to the construction site I was at and told me they were going to search my truck. I said, 'No problem.' A minute later they asked me to come out to my truck. They held up this tire iron and asked if it was mine. I walked over to take a look at it," Craig's emotions began to surface. "There was blood and hair . . ." He was unable to continue. Jeni reached out and covered Craig's trembling hands with her own.

"I showed them where the tire iron for the truck was. I keep it behind the seat in the cab. I was standing there—they were looking at the tire iron from the truck—and I looked at the other tire iron, the one they had. It had white paint on it, so I recognized it." He paused, struggling to remain composed. "It was the tire iron from our Jeep."

Jeni was a little confused. "Do you keep it in your truck?"

"No. The Jeep hasn't run for about four months. As far as I know, it's always been in the Jeep."

"Where is the Jeep now?" Jeni asked.

"It's in the garage at the house."

"Are you sure it's the tire iron from the Jeep?"

"Yeah." Craig rubbed his eyes. "I helped my sister paint her house last summer, and I used the tire iron to pry the lids from the paint cans."

Jeni gathered her thoughts. "Okay. They found it in the back of your truck?"

"Yeah, it was in there with a bunch of my construction tools."

"Do you have any idea how it got there or how long it's been there?" Jeni looked to Craig for an answer.

He thought for a minute. "No, I don't know how it got there. I haven't been to the house since Monday, and I didn't go in the garage that day." He looked up as if he'd just remembered something. "I know it wasn't in the truck Wednesday. I had to take a truckload of brick up to Logan to do some finish work on a home up there. I took most of my tools out and left them in the shed at the office. I didn't put them back in until Saturday morning. I would have noticed it."

Jeni took up her pencil and notepad and began jotting down notes. "Do you know of anyone who would want to frame you? Have you been threatened by anyone?"

"No." Craig shook his head. "I can't think of anyone who would do this."

"Have you had any conflicts with anyone recently, anything significant?"

"No, not that I can think of."

"Has anyone . . ."

Craig interrupted. "Wait. I fired a guy a couple of weeks ago. He'd only worked for me for a couple of months. He didn't show up half the time. The guys told me he had a real drinking problem. But anyway, when I fired him he told me I'd regret it." Craig thought for a moment. "I don't think he'd go this far. I don't know."

"Do you remember his name?"

"Yeah. Darrell Lewis."

Jeni wrote down his name. "Would your office have record of his address and telephone number?"

"Yeah."

"Where is your office located?"

Craig gave Jeni the information she needed.

"I'll give this information to the police and follow up on it myself."

"What happens now?" The worry was evident in Craig's face.

"You'll be arraigned in the morning. I'm not sure what time yet, but I'll find out as soon as I can. The judge will set bail then. I'll do everything I can to get you out of here."

"What about Ryan? I'm not going to lose him, am I?"

"No. Have you made arrangements for someone to watch him?"

"My sister is going to pick him up from daycare and take him to my parents' house. I had her call Mom and ask her if she'd take Ryan for a few days, but I told her to wait and tell her that I was in jail when she got there. She's going to take it pretty hard."

"Your sister's at my office waiting for me. I'll keep in close contact with her." She scribbled her office number and home phone number on the bottom corner of a piece of paper and tore it off. She handed it to Craig. "Here are my phone numbers. They should let you call me if you need to for any reason. If you think of anything that might help us, call. I'll be in court with you in the morning." She looked into Craig's dark, anguished eyes. She wanted so much to reassure him, or perhaps she looked to him, longing for assurance herself. "Everything will be all right. We'll get you through this."

Craig nodded. "Thanks."

Jeni rose and knocked on the door. The guards placed the cuffs and shackles back on their weary prisoner. Jeni put a hand on Craig's shoulder and squeezed gently. "See you in the morning."

*   *   *

Jeni's mind raced as she walked briskly toward her office, oblivious of the people around her. She could not accept the thought that Craig might be guilty. She listed the reasons in her mind for believing in his innocence. He seemed gentle and sincere. Liz had seemed to be comfortable with him and still loved him, despite filing for divorce. Craig appeared to be intelligent, too smart to make the mistakes that had led to his arrest. Jeni was sure Craig was being framed. But by whom? Her thoughts turned to her career. Was she jeopardizing her practice? Was she capable of adequately defending Craig? Was she viewing the situation objectively, or were her emotions overriding her intellect?

The confusion that engulfed Jeni was quickly compounded by guilt. The guilt was due to her intense attraction to her client. She had not been interested in anyone since she and Eric had ended their relationship after two years of dating. That was over three years ago. She questioned her feelings, wondering why she was so taken with this man she hardly knew, this man who was accused of murdering his wife. Jeni's stomach tightened and twisted.

She reached her office building and trotted down the stairs. Danielle Harrison waited on a couch in the reception area and rose anxiously as Jeni walked through the door. Jeni smiled politely. She turned to Kate. "I'll be with Ms. Harrison for a few minutes. When Mr. Degraw gets here would you apologize for me and tell him I'll be with him shortly?"

"You bet." Kate handed Jeni her phone messages.

"Thanks." Jeni looked to Danielle. "Please, come in." Jeni placed her briefcase on the floor and took a seat behind her desk. She looked at the woman who sat across from her. Her beauty was striking; her black hair was thick and curly. It emphasized her dark, captivating eyes. She looked so much like Craig—same eyes, same full lips. Danielle's features were softer, but she shared Craig's olive skin and smooth complexion.

"I think your brother is being framed. Do you know of anyone who would want to do this?" Jeni hoped for an answer that would shed some light on the situation.

Danielle contemplated the question for a moment, then shook her head. "I don't know of anyone who hates Craig."

"I'm going to contact the detective who is investigating Elizabeth's murder. Hopefully, I can convince him that there might be someone out there that would want to hurt Craig badly enough to do this to him. Right now, I only have one lead for him to follow up on, and that's a man Craig fired a few weeks ago." Jeni sighed. "I'm going to need all the information about Craig and the people he associates with that I can get. Can you help me?"

"I'll do anything I can. What do you want to know?"

"I'd like a list of Craig's friends, coworkers, family members, even neighbors he might have been close to. If you could talk with your family, see if anyone knows anything that might help us."

Danielle looked at Jeni with concern. "I'm supposed to leave Thursday for Minneapolis, but I'm trying to postpone my trip for a few days so I can be here for the funeral. I don't know if I'll be able to. I'll be gone for four days, but then I'm going to take a few weeks off. I should be able to help in any way you need me to after this trip. I'll try and get as much information to you as possible before I go."

Jeni had not thought about a funeral. "When will her service be?"

Danielle shifted in her seat. "Liz's mother is handling everything, so all I know is that it will be Thursday morning. I'm not sure what time, but I think she's using Lawson Mortuary. I'm going to call them to see if I can get more information." Danielle's voice cracked with emotion.

"Do you know her mother well?"

"I grew up with Liz. We were best friends from the second grade on. We were pretty much inseparable." Danielle cleared her throat and struggled to remain composed. "My mom was more of a mother to Liz than her own mother was. She was a lot closer to my mom."

"She told the police that she thought Liz was afraid of Craig. Do you know why she would say that?" Jeni asked.

"Well, she never has liked Craig. She didn't think he was good enough for Liz."

Jeni rephrased the question. "Would she have any reason to lie about him to the police?"

"I don't know. I think she just had a certain idea of what Craig was like in her head, and she never got to know him well enough to realize that she was wrong."

"So, she didn't spend a lot of time with Craig and Liz?"

"Oh, no." Danielle shook her head.

"I think the police officers who spoke with her were probably assuming that she and her daughter were close. Maybe it will help if they know that they weren't." Jeni made a mental note to discuss the matter with Detective Lund.

"What about getting Craig out of jail? Can we post bail for him?"

"They won't set bail until he's arraigned in the morning. It's likely to be quite high, considering the charges. I'll do what I can to get a reasonable amount," Jeni answered.

"I'll do whatever it takes to get him out of there." Danielle sounded determined.

"Craig told me you were taking Ryan to your parent's house." Danielle nodded in answer to Jeni's question. "Are you going to tell them about his arrest?"

"Yes."

Jeni rose and reached across her desk, handing Danielle one of her business cards. "Give them my card, and have them call if they need anything at all, or if they want to speak with me for any reason."

"Thank you. I really appreciate everything you're doing for Craig."

Jeni walked out from behind her desk and offered her hand to Danielle. She reassured her that she would do everything she could to get Craig out of jail and prove his innocence.

CHAPTER 11

"Congratulations, Hal." Hal looked up to see Leonard Jarvis approaching his desk.

"Thanks." Hal smiled at his captain.

"There's a reporter at the front desk. He'd like to get a statement on the arrest." Captain Jarvis sat on the corner of Hal's desk. "I'd like to keep this as tight as possible. Just give them the basics, the bare minimum."

Hal nodded. "Can Jim handle this for me?"

"No. I want you dealing with the press. How did it go at the district attorney's office?"

"They were going to go with capital homicide charges, but it would be difficult to prove that the insurance money was a motive. It's going to look to a jury to be more a crime of passion. They're charging him with first-degree murder," Hal explained. "You know," he continued, "our other primary suspect left town in a big hurry last night. Jeffers and Bartholomew drove up to Park City this morning to get him for questioning, and he had skipped town."

"What are you saying? You got your man, don't you?"

Hal, having no explanation as to how the murder weapon could have wound up in Craig Harrison's possession—a man with a motive and no alibi—if he did not do it, nodded. "Looks like it."

"Okay." Jarvis rose and gave Hal a pat on the shoulder. "You did very well, Hal. Would you make sure I've got copies of all the reports?"

"Sure."

"Thanks."

Hal watched Leonard Jarvis walk away. It was rare the captain gave accolades, and normally Hal would be thrilled with the commendation, but Hal was not confident that they had arrested the right person. He had to wonder if his lack of confidence was an overreaction to the mistake he had made on the Archuleta case. No, it was more than that; it was a gut feeling. If he had learned anything from that regrettable incident, it was to follow his instincts.

Hal leaned back in his chair and enjoyed the last of his cigarette before going to the front desk to talk with the reporter. He had yet to meet a reporter he liked and felt no guilt in keeping one waiting. His thoughts went to his wife. Jean had been on his mind all day. He had tried to call her earlier, but she was out of her office. He put his cigarette out and picked up the phone.

"Jean Lund, please," he said when the receptionist answered the phone. He waited for his wife to answer.

"This is Jean."

The sound of Jean's voice put him at ease. "Hi, hun."

"Hi." Jean sounded pleasantly surprised. "What are you doing, calling this time of day?"

"I was hoping to get you to go on a date with me."

"A date?" Jean asked incredulously.

"Yeah. What do you say?"

"Do you know how long it's been since we've been on a date?" Jean asked.

"Let's see, the twenty-fourth of July, when we went out to Wendover."

Jean laughed. "You and your memory."

"So, are you up for dinner at Lorenzo's and maybe dancing afterwards?"

"How can I refuse an offer like that?"

Hal smiled. "Great. I'll pick you up at six."

"I'll believe that when I see it," Jean replied. "You haven't been home from work at six in over a month."

"Well, we made an arrest in the case I'm working on today, and I'm pretty sure I'll be getting off before five-thirty."

"Okay. I'll be ready."

"Good." Hal paused. "Are you doing all right?"

"I'm fine," Jean assured him.

"I'll see you tonight."

"Okay."

"Jeanie, I love you." Hal put the receiver down slowly.

*   *   *

Hal finished fueling his car and slid behind the wheel. The sun was beating down on the windshield, giving more a feeling of midsummer than of autumn. He started the car and turned the air conditioning on, then looked toward the convenience store impatiently. Moments later, Jim sauntered out of the store with an ice-cream bar in one hand and a small bag in the other.

"Did you see that gal in there?" Jim asked as his bulk settled into the car. Hal shook his head. "Whew! She couldn't have been more than nineteen. Had a body she should register as a lethal weapon!" He shook his head. "Man!"

As Hal drove out of the parking lot, he looked over his shoulder at the woman behind the counter in the store. "You've been alone for too long, buddy!" he laughed.

"Hey, she looked good," Jim defended himself. "You've just been married too long."

"Did you get a receipt for the gas?" Hal asked.

Jim devoured half of the chocolate-coated ice-cream bar in one bite. "Yeah," he said as ice cream dribbled down his chin. He reached into his jacket pocket and pulled out a receipt.

"Just put it in there." Hal motioned to the glove compartment.

Jim finished off the ice-cream bar and licked the stick before tossing it in the bag next to him. "Speaking of good-looking women," he looked at Hal and raised his eyebrows, "that lawyer lady wasn't bad."

"You mean Harrison's lawyer?"

"Yeah. What a babe!" Jim rubbed the back of his neck. "Mmm, mmm, mmm. She had legs that went on forever. Enough to make a grown man cry, isn't it?"

"Maybe a pathetically lonely one like you." Hal smiled.

"Yeah, tell me you wouldn't want those legs wrapped around your waist!"

That comment riled Hal. "Would you shut up?" He had thought Jenifer Sullivan was an extremely attractive woman and in one of his weaker moments had thought of her legs in such a position, but it was not something he was proud of or allowed himself to dwell on. That was not the only reason Jim's remark had bothered him. It brought up a feeling of guilt over the thoughts he had entertained of leaving Jean.

"Hey!" Jim yelled. "Where ya goin'? It's right there." Jim pointed to the Little Willow Daycare Center.

"Shit!" Hal looked behind him to see if it was clear and slammed on the brakes. He barely made the turn into the driveway.

Jim extracted himself from the car and fell in behind Hal. "And you talk about the way I drive!"

Hal ignored Jim's complaints and entered the daycare center.

A young woman holding an infant waded through a noisy sea of children and approached the two policemen. "Can I help you?"

Hal stepped forward. "Yes. I'm Sergeant Lund, with the Salt Lake Police. This is Officer Webber." Hal gestured to Jim, who nodded and smiled.

"Oh, yes. I spoke with you on the phone. I'm Lisa Bowen." The woman gently bounced the baby as she spoke.

"Could we take a moment of your time and have you answer a few more questions for us?" Hal asked.

"Sure. Let me get Kari in here to watch the kids for me for a minute." The woman disappeared into another room and emerged with another woman. She handed the infant to the woman and joined Hal and Jim. "Why don't we go in here," she said, motioning toward an adjoining room.

Hal and Jim followed Lisa into a small kitchen. "We can sit down, if you'd like." She closed the door and walked toward a table that was surrounded by chairs.

Hal took a seat at the table and opened his note-book. "How long have you known Elizabeth Harrison?"

"Oh, let's see. She's been bringing Ryan here since he was three. So, about a year and a half."

"Did she ever talk to you about her marriage?" Hal tugged at his mustache as he waited for the woman to answer.

"No." Lisa shook her head. "We mostly talked about Ryan. She was never here for more than a few minutes at a time."

"Did you ever meet her husband?" Jim asked.

"Oh, yes. He would drop Ryan off almost as often as Liz would. In fact, he brought Ryan by this morning."

Hal looked up from his notebook in surprise. "He was here this morning?"

"Yes, just after eight," Lisa replied.

"So, Ryan is here," Hal asserted.

Lisa shook her head. "Craig's sister came by and picked him up about twenty minutes ago."

Hal looked at his partner, contemplating his next question, then turned back to Lisa. "What is your impression of Mr. Harrison and his relationship with his wife?"

Lisa shrugged her shoulders. "I don't know. He's very nice. Verrrry good-looking," She beamed. "I never saw the two of them together. Either one or the other of them dropped Ryan off or picked him up." She paused. "He's a nice guy."

"Mrs. Harrison dropped Ryan off the morning she was murdered, Tuesday the twenty-first. Is that correct?"

The mention of the murder sobered Lisa's disposition. "Yes," she answered Hal in a quiet voice.

Hal continued his questions. "Did she mention that she was going to Park City or say anything about her husband?"

"No. She didn't say anything."

"And her mother picked Ryan up that afternoon, correct?"

Lisa nodded. "Yes."

"Her mother's done this before?" Jim asked.

"Yeah, a couple of times," Lisa replied.

"Okay," Hal leaned forward, "so as far as you know the Harrison's marriage was good?"

"They both seemed to be happy, if that's what you mean. But, like I said, we really only talked about Ryan."

Hal closed his notebook and placed the pen back in his pocket. "We appreciate you talking with us, Miss Bowen." He stood and pushed in his chair.

"I don't know how she can do that," Jim said as he and Hal walked toward their car.

"Do what?"

"Take care of all those kids. I mean, being around your own kids is one thing, but somebody else's? I couldn't do it."

Hal opened his door and looked across the top of the car at his partner. "You were never around your own kids."

Jim got in the car. "I brought in a paycheck every month. I put braces on their teeth and paid for their little league."

"Too bad you missed their games."

"You know, my ex gives me enough grief. I don't need parenting lessons or morals lectures from you." Jim was offended.

"I'm sorry. I didn't mean anything, big guy," Hal apologized.

"Ah, that's okay. You're right." Jim stared out the window. "Some things you just don't realize until it's too late."

Hal nodded in agreement. Jim's words hit home.

* * *

Jean was in front of the bathroom mirror, donning a pair of earrings, when she heard Hal pull into the driveway. She glanced at her watch. It was ten minutes past six. She smiled.

"Honey?" Hal called from the hallway.

Jean walked out and greeted Hal. "I can't believe you actually made it."

"Hey, I would have been here half an hour ago, but I stopped by to get these." He handed Jean two long-stemmed red roses. "Wow, you look great!"

Jean stared at the flowers in disbelief. "Call 911! I think I'm going into shock."

"Hey, I've given you flowers before." Hal put his arms around his wife.

Jean grinned. "Let's see, I think you did buy me a corsage for our senior prom." The two of them laughed. "I'll get these in a vase."

"Okay. I'm just going to change real quick, and then we'll go." Hal slipped into the bedroom and exchanged his blue suit for a pair of black slacks and a black and tan dress shirt. He took a small comb from his pocket and ran it through his hair. As he combed his hair back, he noticed that his hairline was slowly getting farther and farther away from his brow. He parted his hair and combed it toward one side. He studied the new style in the mirror before combing it back in the usual manner.

"Are you finally ready?" Jean asked as she walked into the room.

"Yeah," Hal answered, studying his waistline in the mirror.

"You look fine, Hal."

"I look old." He turned to Jean. "You're married to an old man."

"I'm sure married to a sexy old man, though." Jean gave Hal's rear end a pinch.

"Hey!"

Jean told Hal the latest gossip from her office as they drove to the restaurant. She explained how her supervisor had announced her engagement to a man twelve years her junior. It was the consensus of the bank's staff that he was basically a lazy punk who wanted a free ride. "Of course, nobody's going to tell Sally that," Jean added as Hal pulled into a parking space.

"Of course not." Hal rolled his eyes. He held his wife's hand as they walked from the parking lot. "Boy, it sure is changing down here." He looked around him at the core of the city.

"Yeah, it really is," Jean agreed.

"You know, they're going to tear that down and put up a new convention center." Hal pointed across the street to the Salt Palace.

"They can't tear that down!" Jean looked at Hal. "That's Salt Lake's trademark."

"It won't be any longer."

"Really?" Jean had a hard time believing it.

"Really. We've seen a lot of things in that old place, haven't we?"

Jean tossed her head back and laughed. "Remember when we saw Glen Campbell there?"

"Yeah." Hal chuckled. "That girl with the hair down past her waist sat in front of us." Jean broke into uncontrollable laughter. As her giggling subsided, she wiped the tears from her eyes. "You sat down after that standing ovation and her head . . ." She laughed again. "Her head snapped back so hard."

Hal smiled and shook his head. "I'll never forget that."

"I don't know how you managed to get her hair caught in your zipper. Oh, my God, that was funny." Jean grabbed Hal's arm and put her head on his shoulder.

"Remember the first time I took you to a hockey game there?"

"The first and last, you mean." Jean smiled. "I can't believe they're going to tear it down."

"Yeah, it's kind of like losing an old friend, huh?" Hal asked.

"Well, like when they tore the Terrace down. Remember when we'd go dancing there almost every weekend?"

Hal nodded. "That was before the kids were born, though."

"I haven't thought about the old days for so long." She thought for a moment. "Remember that greasy little restaurant we'd always eat at?"

"Grant's?"

"Yeah, that's it."

"It's still there," Hal said.

"No!"

"Yeah, it is."

Jean stopped just outside of Lorenzo's. "Why don't we go there? For old time's sake."

Hal looked at his wife. "Are you serious?"

"Yeah, why not?"

He smiled. "Okay. We might need a tetanus shot afterwards, but what the hell." The two turned around and walked the three blocks to Grant's, arm in arm. The sun hovered over the salt flats to the west, splashing the Salt Lake City skyline with brilliant streaks of orange and gold. The sounds of the traffic echoed, bouncing between man-made mountains of concrete, steel and glass. A young couple cuddled close together in a horse-drawn carriage waved as they passed. And in the distance, the tabernacle bells could be heard.

Grant's Diner was sandwiched between a one-hour photo lab and a pawnshop. Hal held the door for his wife. They took a seat in a booth near the door. Jean looked around in amazement. "It hasn't changed much, has it?"

"No. In fact, I think that gravy I spilled last time we were here is still on this seat." Hal took a napkin from the dispenser on the table and dabbed at the bench. "What are you going to get?"

"You know, I think I'm going to forget my diet and get a burger and fries," Jean replied.

"You should forget your diet anyway. You don't need to lose any weight. You're thin!"

"And the reason I'm thin, dear, is because I diet. I have to work at keeping it that way, you know."

Hal thought for a moment. "I guess I kind of take it for granted that I can eat what I want and pretty much stay the same. Although my belts are starting to feel a little tighter these days."

A middle-aged waitress approached the table. "What'll it be?" she asked in a voice husky from cigarettes.

"Two deluxe burgers with fries." Hal handed the menus to the woman.

"Anything to drink?"

"I'll just have water," Jean answered.

"Coke, please." Hal smiled at the woman. He watched her walk away. "Boy, she loves her job, huh?" His tone was sarcastic.

"Tell me about this case you're working on." Jean looked to Hal with interest.

"It's the woman who was killed last week."

"I thought so," Jean said. "You made an arrest today?"

"Yeah, we arrested the husband." Hal rubbed his chin. "Jeanie," he shook his head, "I don't think he did it."

"So why did you arrest him?"

"Well, we found the murder weapon in his truck," Hal answered.

"But you don't think he did it." Jean seemed confused.

Hal sighed. "I don't know. It's just what my gut says. I think she was having an affair." He thought for a moment. "Maybe she wasn't. Maybe somebody really hates her husband and wants to frame him." He shrugged his shoulders. "Maybe he did it. Bonner and Jarvis are ready to close the case, but I'm not."

"Two burgers," the waitress announced as she placed the meals on the table. "I'll be back with your Coke."

When the woman left the table Hal leaned toward his wife. "Was that a promise or a threat?" The two laughed. They continued reminiscing over old times, sharing memories they had not discussed in years.

                    *   *   *

After a slow, leisurely walk back to their car, Hal drove toward the east side of town. "Where are we going?" Jean asked.

"I've got something I want to show you." Hal smiled like a child with a treasured secret.

He turned east off Foothill Drive and drove to a cul-de-sac where a few new homes were being built. He pulled up to the curb and shut the engine off. "Look at that view!"

Jean looked out her window at the sea of sparkling lights below them. She could see the water tower at Trolley Square, the Salt Palace drum, the LDS Temple and the lights of Capitol Hill. The twinkling beams stretched from the mountain behind the capitol building to the Oquirrh Mountains across the valley to the west. It was breathtaking. "It's beautiful!" she exclaimed.

"How would you like to look out the kitchen window and see that view?"

Jean turned to Hal. "What are you saying?"

Hal slid closer to his wife and put his arm around her shoulders. "I'm saying that I've priced the property up here, and I think we should sell the house and build us a home right here."

"You're serious, aren't you?"

"Dead serious." Hal looked deeply into Jean's soft green eyes. "What do you think?"

"I don't know." Jean seemed overwhelmed by the notion. "How long have you been thinking about this?"

"I've toyed with the idea of building a new house for the past year or so. I just called on this property this morning."

"You really think we could afford it?" Jean looked back out over the city below them, then at the surrounding neighborhood. "It's really nice, Hal."

"Of course we can afford it. Now that the kids are gone we don't need all that much space, just a nice little two- or three-bedroom home. Two-car garage, bay window in front, sun porch and deck out back." He touched upon the things he knew his wife had wanted.

"Oh, Hal, it sounds wonderful!"

"So, should we do it?" Hal asked with anticipation.

"Do we have to rush into this?"

"This property will go fast, babe. Besides, why wait?"

"I don't know." Jean was apprehensive. "It's just so sudden."

"Jean, we're not getting any younger. We've got to pursue our dreams. We've got to find the things we want in life and make them happen for us. Why wait?" Hal was desperate to view the future, now that it was being threatened. He fought to ease his fears with concrete plans that cemented their eventuality, as though they would somehow guarantee that he and Jean would grow old together.

"Okay. If we look at our finances and the market for our house looks promising, I'm willing."

Hal's lips curved upward in a broad smile. "I love you." He leaned over and pressed his lips gently against Jean's soft mouth. As their kisses grew longer and deeper, a passion was stirred within Hal that he had not felt for a long time.

CHAPTER 12

It was usually eight when Jeni left for work, but after a rough night with very little sleep, she was up and on her way just after seven. Traffic was light, and Jeni traveled the three miles to her office in a matter of minutes. She locked the door behind her and made her way to her desk. Sitting down in her high-back leather chair with a sigh, she opened the morning paper. Jeni turned immediately to the local section, curious to see if Craig's arrest had been reported.

"Husband Charged in Murder." The headline glared from the bottom corner of the front page. Jeni read on. "Craig Harrison, 30, was arrested early Tuesday and charged with murdering his wife of eight years, Elizabeth Harrison. Mrs. Harrison's body was found Sunday in Emigration Canyon. She had been bludgeoned to death earlier in the week. It is speculated that Mr. Harrison, despondent over their upcoming divorce, attacked his wife after an argument. Sergeant Harold Lund of the Salt Lake City Police Department declined to release any further details regarding Mrs. Harrison's murder.

Mr. Harrison is due to be arraigned in circuit court this morning."

Jeni put the paper down. She wondered if Sergeant Lund had told the reporter about the supposed argument, or if that had come from another source. She had stayed awake the night before, plagued with the fear that she was going into this case blinded by her powerful attraction to the client she was to defend. The possibility that he could be deceiving her with his quiet charm disturbed her. Things were not always as they appeared, Jeni reminded herself.

Jeni pushed the thoughts from her mind. She considered herself a good judge of character, and in talking with Elizabeth, Craig and his sister, she had been given no reason to doubt that Craig was a decent, hardworking man who really did love his wife. Ultimately, Jeni knew that having accepted the case she was bound by her professional honor to defend her client and do her best to represent his interests. Why was she haunted by these doubts? She was disappointed by her inability to shut them out.

She took out her notes and looked over the information she had gathered regarding the case. She made a list of contacts to make and information she still needed. She was anxious to talk with whomever was handling the case for the district attorney's office. She wanted to know what evidence they had collected against Craig Harrison.

          *   *   *

The elevator doors opened, and Jeni stepped out to find Danielle Harrison waiting for her. She was striking, dressed in a black shirt and slacks and a red suit jacket. As Danielle approached, she was followed by a tall, well-built gentleman with graying hair and two women. The older of the two women was dark and attractive, having the same deep-set brown eyes as both Danielle and Craig. The younger woman was quite tall, and her shoulders were exceptionally broad for a woman. Though her build was considerably masculine, her soft blonde hair and sparkling blue eyes made her attractive. Jeni guessed her to be in her early thirties.

Jeni greeted Danielle with a firm handshake. "Good morning."

Danielle turned to the couple behind her. "These are my parents, Frank and Linda Harrison." She motioned back to Jeni. "This is Jenifer Sullivan, Craig's attorney."

"Mrs. Harrison," Jeni said as she shook the woman's hand. "Mr. Harrison. It's very nice to meet you both." Both Mr. and Mrs. Harrison appeared tired and distraught.

Danielle turned to her right. "This is Robin Curtis." The woman smiled politely and extended her hand.

"I'm very glad you could all be here," Jeni began. "The more support we can give Craig, the more support we can show the court he has, the better we can help him." Jeni noticed an empty couch near the window in the waiting area. "Why don't we sit down."

Mrs. Harrison dabbed her eyes with a handkerchief. "We'll do anything we can to help Craig. We know he's innocent. We know he didn't do this." She continued, "We'll put our house up for collateral, if necessary, to get him out."

"Well, pooling of your financial resources and properties might be necessary. Right now, what I'd like you all to concentrate on is establishing character witnesses, helping us prove his alibi, and finding any leads for us to follow," Jeni said. "We also have to focus on being positive. We have to believe we can prove Craig's innocence."

"What's going to happen in court?" Mr. Harrison asked.

"He'll be arraigned today, which means they'll formally level charges against him and allow him to enter an initial plea. After he enters that plea, the judge can decide whether or not to allow bail, and at what amount." Jeni noticed David Crandall, with whom she had worked at the district attorney's office, exiting the elevator and walking toward the courtroom. "If you'll excuse me for a moment."

"Dave!" she called out as he was about to enter the courtroom.

He turned and his face broke into a broad grin when he saw Jeni. "Hi! How you doin'?"

"Good. How are you?"

"Not bad."

"I didn't know you were handling felonies now."

David beamed. "I just started about a month ago."

"Wow, that's great," Jeni said. "Hey, I'm defending Craig Harrison, the murder-one charge. Would you mind slipping into the conference room for a minute to discuss it with me?"

"I'd love to, but I'm not handling it."

"Oh. Who is?"

"Arthur Jackson."

The name set off a ringing in Jeni's head, like a fire alarm that refused to shut off. It took her a moment to recover from the initial shock. "Arthur Jackson?" she asked, hoping she had heard him wrong.

"Yeah. Taylor was going to take it, but Jackson threw his weight around, 'cause I guess he really wanted this one."

This was a twist Jeni had not expected. Her heart seemed to sink to the depths of her stomach, then flutter slowly back into her chest. Her daze was disrupted by David Crandall's voice. "Jen? Are you all right?"

Jeni tried to shake the sick feeling that had subdued her. "Yes, I'm sorry."

"Well, I've got to get in there. I have to get some things from the clerk. It's good to see you." David smiled.

"Good seeing you." Bewildered, Jeni walked back to where the Harrisons were sitting.

Danielle spoke as Jeni approached. "When will Craig be getting here?"

"They'll probably bring him a few minutes before court starts at eight-thirty. They have tunnels that go from the jail over here to the courthouse. They'll bring

him through the back of the courtroom and seat him in
the jury box." She paused. "You won't be able to have
any contact with him in there. I suggest . . ." Jeni
stopped in mid-sentence, halted by a low, deep laugh
that was chillingly familiar. She turned and looked over
her shoulder. Her eyes fell upon a short, stocky man in
a gray pinstriped suit. His eyes were a steely blue, his
thin lips shaded by a sparse gray mustache, his head
covered with an obtrusive hair piece. It was the first
time she had seen Arthur Jackson since leaving the
district attorney's office. The animosity had not dimin-
ished.

Jeni turned back to the Harrisons, trying to hide the
fact that she was flustered. "I suggest that you not try to
speak with him until afterward. I'll see if I can get them
to let you speak with him then." She looked at her
watch. "I'd better get in there."

As she walked past Arthur Jackson, she felt a
shudder run through her flesh. She avoided looking at
him, hoping he had not noticed her. Her hopes were in
vain.

"Well, Mizzz Sullivan." He walked away from the
man he was talking to and caught up to Jeni. "We meet
again."

Jeni looked up at him, hoping the trembling she felt
throughout her body was not noticeable. "Mr. Jackson."
Her tone was abrupt.

"I hear you're defending this murder case." He
produced a malevolent smirk. "You want to play with

the big boys, huh?" Jeni started to walk away. "You'll get eaten alive, sweetheart."

As Jeni entered the courtroom, a group of inmates were filing into the jury box. Craig Harrison looked out of place among the disheveled-looking, unshaven, tattooed men. His conspicuous uniform seemed to be the only similarity. Jeni nodded to him as he noticed her. She placed her briefcase on the defense table and approached the jury box.

"How are you feeling today?" She gave a confident smile.

"Nervous," Craig fidgeted in obvious discomfort. His hands remained cuffed behind his back.

Jeni turned to one of the officers who had escorted the prisoners into the courtroom. "Can we get these handcuffs removed?"

"I'm sorry, ma'am. We can take them off just before he goes before the judge, but not before. It's policy now." The man seemed sincerely apologetic.

Jeni nodded in compliance, then looked to Craig. "I'm sorry."

"It's okay."

"When they call your name, you'll go over there to that podium." She pointed to a small stand in front of the judge's bench. "He'll explain the charges against you. When he asks how you plead say, 'Not guilty.' I'll discuss bail with the judge at that time. If you have anything to say at any time, just lean over and tell me. Okay?"

"Yeah."

Jeni had waited to discuss Craig's case with Arthur Jackson until they were in the courtroom, where his remarks would hopefully be kept professional. She approached the prosecution table where Jackson sat talking with David Crandall. "Mr. Jackson, I would like to discuss the State's position in the case against my client, Craig Harrison."

"Well, Miss Sullivan, considering the sensitivity involved in this case, I think it's crucial that the prosecution withhold most information from the defense," he replied condescendingly.

Jeni's ire began to rise, but she kept her temper in check. "You're obligated to provide the defense with appropriate information."

"Let's see, if you had done your homework, you'd find that Utah Code, section seventy-seven, chapter twenty-two, paragraph one allows the prosecution to withhold information. I would suggest you read it." Arthur Jackson turned away after delivering the advice.

"Please rise." The court clerk entered the room and made the request of those in attendance. She went on to declare court in session and announce the presiding judge. Jeni sat next to an attorney from the legal defenders' office and watched the first three arraignments.

"Next case is three—two—nine—eight—nine—four, State versus Craig Michael Harrison," the judge announced.

A guard helped Craig from his seat and removed his restraints. Jeni's nervousness disappeared as she stepped up to the podium next to her client. This was a comfort zone for her. She was well acquainted with the judge and familiar with his proclivities. Arthur Jackson was intimidating, but Jeni's self-confidence was little shaken. The court clerk rose and spoke directly to Craig. "State your full name and address for the court."

Craig cleared his throat. "Craig Michael Harrison, 1251 Kraft Street."

The judge looked over the information before him, then raised his eyes toward Craig. "Mr. Harrison, you're represented by counsel?"

"Yes, sir."

The judge looked at Jeni. "Do you want the information read?"

"No, Your Honor."

"The defendant waives the reading of the information." The judge pivoted in his seat and leaned back with his fingers to his chin. "Mr. Harrison, you are charged with murder in the first degree in the death of Elizabeth Connor Harrison. This is a first-degree felony punishable by a prison term not less than five years and not to exceed life." He paused. "Do you understand the seriousness of this charge, Mr. Harrison?"

"Yes, sir."

"Mr. Harrison, to the charge of first-degree murder, how do you plead?"

"Not guilty, Your Honor." Craig maintained constant eye contact with the judge.

"Mr. Jackson," the judge turned to Arthur Jackson, "does the State have any objections to bail being allowed in this case?"

"Your Honor," Arthur Jackson stepped out from behind the prosecution table and approached the bench, "the State has no objection to bail being set, but we would ask that the amount be not less than five hundred thousand dollars."

The judge looked back to Jeni. "Ms. Sullivan?"

"Thank you, Your Honor. My client has never been arrested previous to this incident. He owns and operates a construction business here in Salt Lake City. He has a home here, a four-year-old son living with him, and his extended family lives here in the area. Considering his lack of a prior record, his business, his ties to this community, his responsibilities as a father, and his family's support, I would ask for a reduced bail."

"Mr. Jackson?" the judge turned back to Arthur.

"As I stated earlier, the State feels the seriousness of the charge warrants an excessive bail."

The judge pondered over the circumstances for a long moment before speaking. "The court will remand the defendant to remain in the custody of the Salt Lake County Jail and will set bail in the amount of one hundred thousand dollars." He rubbed his chin with his fingers and looked intently at Craig. "Mr. Harrison, you understand that if you are able to post bail, you will remain under the jurisdiction of this court and will not be allowed to leave the area?"

"Yes, sir."

"That will be the order of the court." He swiveled around to face the court clerk to his right. "When is the next available date for a preliminary hearing?"

The clerk looked over the calendar. "October twenty-sixth."

"We'll set a preliminary hearing in this case for October the twenty-sixth at eight a.m." He paused. "Set aside two days for that." The judge picked up the file for the next case.

Jeni walked Craig back to the jury box where the officers waited for him. "I'll come by the jail in about an hour to talk with you. We'll see what we can do about raising bail."

"Thanks." Craig's expression remained sullen.

*   *   *

The cool air that greeted Jeni as she stepped from the court building was refreshing. She walked down the steps, lamenting the fact that she was wearing heels. Her feet seemed to be the focal point of her increasing fatigue. As she walked across the quad that sat amid the circuit and district courthouses, the Salt Lake Public Library and the Salt Lake County Jail, Jeni thought of Arthur Jackson. Memories of her confrontations with him came streaming back to her.

Arthur Jackson was the Chief Assistant District Attorney. He had been with the district attorney's office for seventeen years. He was an immutable fixture there. When Jeni started working in the office as a law clerk, Arthur Jackson told her that he could pull some strings and get her a position on the legal staff if she would "loosen up and become a little friendlier" with him. Jeni declined his offer and continued to work hard while she finished her last years of law school at the University of Utah. When she was hired on as an attorney following her graduation, Jackson threatened to get her fired if she mentioned his earlier advances and made offers of raises and promotions in return for sex. Jeni ignored the harassment at first, but when talking turned to groping and it became an almost daily occurrence, she went to her supervisor and filed a complaint. The complaint fell on deaf ears. Six months later, she left the district attorney's office.

Defending Craig Harrison was itself an imposing challenge but with Arthur Jackson acting as prosecution in the case it would be an arduous task. Uneasiness was replaced with determination as Jeni vowed to herself to prove her abilities as a trial lawyer to the man who had promised to ruin her career. Her pace quickened with this newly found resolve as she neared the entrance to the jail.

After waiting ten minutes, Jeni was escorted by an officer to a visiting room. Another ten minutes passed before they brought Craig down from his cell. As the guards removed the handcuffs from his outstretched arms, Jeni noticed the solid muscles that bulged beneath his sleeves. Her eyes followed the span of his shoulders and descended across the ripples of his chest and abdomen. Her momentary lapse into unprofessionalism shamed her, and she quickly focused on the questions she had jotted down in her notebook.

"I spoke with your parents and your sister after court. They're working on getting a bond for you. Hopefully, we'll have you out sometime this afternoon."

"Really?" Craig's face showed a glimmer of hope.

Jeni nodded. "Now, I'm going to have to do a little investigative work. We have to find some way to prove your alibi." Seeing no response from Craig, she continued. "Tell me again what you did last Tuesday."

Craig took a deep breath. "Well, I was at the office until a little before one. I was supposed to meet Dave

Mansfield in Vernal at four-thirty. When I left the office, I stopped and got gas . . ."

"Wait. Why did you have this meeting with Mr. Mansfield?" Jeni asked.

"He's doing some cement work on a home I'll be building there. He called and asked if I could look at the property before he pours the foundation. He had some questions about drainage—some stuff that could pose problems for us later on."

"Okay, go ahead."

"I got gas in the truck, stopped at the apartment and changed my shirt, and headed to Vernal. I got there about four-thirty, drove to the lot, and waited." Craig shrugged his shoulders. "I waited for about thirty or forty minutes and then drove into town and found a pay phone and called him. There wasn't an answer, so I drove back over to the lot and waited until about quarter to six. He never showed."

Jeni was writing down Craig's explanation. "Then where did you go?"

"I was getting hungry. I only had about five dollars, so I found an ATM and got some cash. Then I went to McDonald's, ate, and drove home."

"What time was it when you got home?"

"A little after ten."

"Did you ever find out where Mr. Mansfield was?" Jeni asked.

"Well, the next morning when I went to the office, my secretary told me he had called just before she went to lunch Tuesday, about noon. He told her he had to leave town and wouldn't be able to meet with me. She said she left the message on my desk, but I never got it." Craig shook his head.

Jeni wrote his reply down. "Can you think of anyone who could place you there? Did you talk with anyone you think might remember you?"

"The only person that I talked to was the girl at McDonald's, and I can't even remember what she looked like." Craig brought his hand up and caressed his forehead as if he suddenly had a headache.

"I'll see what I can come up with." Jeni gathered her notebook and stood. "I hate to run off, but I have appointments waiting. I'll be in touch with you this afternoon." She knocked on the door. "Hopefully, it won't be in here."

CHAPTER 13

The sky over Salt Lake City was bleak. Thick clouds hung low, not threatening rain, but impeding the rays of the morning sun, thwarting its warmth and light. Jeni pulled into the Salt Lake City Cemetery and followed the markers to Elizabeth Harrison's services. She pulled her Grand Prix up behind a row of cars and shut off the engine. She sat for a moment, watching people gather around a casket that sat at the edge of an open grave, surrounded by floral arrangements.

The gathering was small. Jeni guessed the group to be about thirty in number. She took a deep breath as she prepared to get out of her car and join the assembly of mourners. She felt out of place, hardly knowing the woman who was about to be laid to rest. But Jeni had been drawn here by her profound desire to learn about this woman whose death had become such a significant part of her life, occupying a great deal of her time and energy.

She stepped from her car and stopped to straighten her dress. She saw Danielle and the woman she had introduced her to at the courthouse, standing near Craig and a little boy she assumed was Ryan. She walked up the sloping lawn, noticing the sound of the leaves crackling beneath her feet. She could see people's lips moving, as if they were talking to each other, but silence hung heavy and Jeni could hear no voices. She walked up behind Craig and put a gentle hand on his shoulder. He turned and captured the words that were about to leave her lips. Her thoughts escaped her, taken away by Craig's captivating presence. His thick, black hair curled over the collar of a dark gray suit. His eyes were warm and intense.

After a moment, Craig broke the awkward silence. "Ms. Sullivan, I appreciate you coming."

Jeni, embarrassed by her speechlessness, blushed. "Please, call me Jenifer." She paused. "I just want to offer my condolences."

"Thank you."

The little boy clinging to Craig looked up at him. "Daddy, that hole's so deep."

Craig bent down and picked the boy up. The resemblance was evident. The little boy's hair was lighter, his features more angled; but the eyes were his father's. "Ryan, this is Jenifer. She's a friend of your Dad's. She's a very nice lady." The boy looked at Jeni, then turned his eyes away in shyness. Craig beamed with pride. "This is my son, Ryan."

"Hi, Ryan. It's nice to meet you. You're sure a handsome young man."

Ryan smiled. He turned to his father. "Daddy, that big hole over there, is that where they're going to put Mommy?" Craig's face quickly became pained. It was obvious that he was unsure how to answer his son's question. "She won't be able to breathe in there," Ryan worried aloud.

"It's just Mommy's body that they're going to put in there. Her spirit is up in heaven," Craig explained.

"Is she an angel?" Ryan played with Craig's tie as he talked.

A tear formed in Craig's eye and slowly forged its way down his cheek. "Yes, son, Mommy's an angel."

"Oh, my God!" a slender, silver-haired woman exclaimed as she approached the grave site. "What is he doing here?" She stared at Craig in disbelief. She was quickly taken to the opposite side of the gathering by the two men who had escorted her there.

"Gramma!" Ryan called out.

There was a deadening silence as everyone turned to see what the commotion was over. Danielle leaned over and whispered in Jeni's ear. "That's Liz's mother."

Jeni was surprised by Helen Connor's appearance, though she had not really given any conscious thought to how she might look. She was impeccably dressed and carried herself well.

"Daddy, can I see Gramma?" Ryan asked Craig.

Craig set his son on the ground. "Yeah." Ryan ran over to Helen Connor with outstretched arms. Helen bent down and talked to the boy in a quiet voice.

Danielle turned to her brother. "I can imagine what she's telling him about you." Craig said nothing in reply.

An elderly couple approached Craig. The woman, tears streaming down her face, hugged him, offering her sympathies. Jeni stood back and watched Craig and his family interact with the others in attendance.

Before long, a representative of the mortuary stepped forward and welcomed everyone to the grave-side services for Elizabeth Connor Harrison. He then introduced Elizabeth's uncle, Martin Connor, who gave a brief eulogy. He talked of Elizabeth's love for her son, her willingness to serve others, her quiet demeanor. He spoke of her death as a tragic loss and articulated the void that her family and friends would always feel. A dedicatory prayer was offered by another uncle, and then the service was concluded.

Jeni was surprised at the brevity of the ceremony. Most of the guests appeared to be either friends or members of Craig's family. Helen Connor sat on a chair next to Elizabeth's casket and wept quietly. She left immediately after the service. Craig, his parents, Danielle and her younger brother watched as the cemetery workers lowered Elizabeth's coffin into the ground. Jeni was touched as she watched Craig help Ryan take a yellow rose from a colorful spray and place it in the grave.

Jeni walked over to tell Craig and Danielle she was leaving. Before she reached them, Craig had walked with his parents to their car.

"Take all the time you need." Robin Curtis gave Danielle a hug. "I'll be in the car." Robin walked away, leaving Danielle standing over Liz's grave.

"I know this is hard for you. Losing a loved one is hard in itself, and you have all this added pain. I just want to offer my sympathies." Jeni paused. "I'll be in touch with you." She turned to walk away.

"Liz would appreciate all you're doing for Craig." Her voice cracked with emotion. "Thank you for coming."

"I came because I wanted to learn more about Liz, but I'm afraid I don't know much more than I did before. Someday, maybe you can tell me about her."

Danielle seemed surprised by Jeni's statement. She wiped the tears from her face and bowed her head. "It's really too bad you didn't have the opportunity to know Liz while she was still with us." She took a deep breath and let it out slowly. "She was an amazing person. She was the kind of friend most people only wish they had. She was always there for me." The tears began flowing faster. "She loved sunsets and the smell of fresh-cut grass. She loved iced tea and ate her cold cereal from the box. She had the most beautiful voice." She shook her head. "You know, very few people know that about her. She plays the guitar and sings. She's really wonderful." She spoke of Elizabeth briefly as though she were still alive. "She wanted to be a fireman when she was a little girl. When we got into high school, she decided she wanted to be a teacher. Whatever she was doing, it was something that would help people."

There was a silence. "She sounds very special," Jeni said.

"She was so caring. And funny." Danielle laughed through her tears. "Oh, she could make me laugh like nobody else could." Danielle seemed lost in memories. After a few moments, she spoke again. "Her favorite color was blue. She loved Italian food. Katherine Hepburn was her hero. Her favorite singer was Ann Wilson. Her favorite time of year was spring. She loved old musicals and good books, and fancied herself a poet at times." Danielle looked at the sky. "On a day like today, she would make hot chocolate and stay inside and play with Ryan or play board games with anyone she could rope into it." Danielle dabbed her eyes dry with a tissue. "More than anything, Liz just wanted everyone to be happy. A lot of times she sacrificed her own happiness, trying to be what she thought everyone else wanted her to be."

Jeni looked down at Elizabeth's casket and was overcome with sorrow. This person Danielle spoke so lovingly of was lying lifeless there, the tragic victim of needless violence. The need to know who was responsible for this death intensified. Jeni put her arm around Danielle and gave a gentle squeeze. "Remember her life; it was obviously a beautiful one."

"Thanks."

Jeni walked to her car and got in. As she drove out of the cemetery, she passed another funeral service in progress. She wondered who it was that was being buried there and whose lives that person had touched. She felt vulnerable, temporal and unmistakably mortal.

CHAPTER 14

"We're going to be late!" Jim looked at Hal impatiently.

"I've never met a lawyer yet who's on time. Relax." Hal continued filling out the paperwork that sat neglected on his desk for the past three days.

"Yeah, well, I've got a life, too, you know. Can we just get this over with?"

Hal dropped his pen. "Hey, why didn't you tell me?"

"Tell you what?" Jim was growing irritated.

"That you got a life. I had no idea." Hal grinned facetiously.

"Kiss my ass!"

Hal enjoyed a good laugh before getting up and donning his jacket. "Okay, let's go."

Jim shook his head as they exited their office. "I don't know why I take this crap from you."

Hal gave Jim a pat on the shoulder. "Deep down you know you enjoy it."

"Yeah, right." Jim rolled his eyes.

Hal opened the door leading outside and held it for his partner. "So, what's up with you?" He was genuinely concerned.

"Whaddya mean?"

"Well, you just seem a little uptight today." Hal and Jim started across the street.

Jim shrugged his shoulders. "My daughter called me last night."

"Which one?" Hal asked.

"Julie." Jim waited until they reached the other side of the intersection to continue. "She's getting married."

"Julie?" Hal was surprised. "Last time I saw her she was only this big." Hal held his hand about four feet off the ground, indicating her height. "Who's she going to marry?"

"She's met a kid at school. He's a junior. His name's Mike Burack, or something like that."

"Is he from here?" Hal asked.

"No, California."

Hal thought for a minute. "So, is it just the fact that your daughter's getting married, or what? What's bothering you about it?"

"The wedding is November fifth. They've been engaged for about two months. Last night is the first I've heard about it. I talked to Arlene last week, and she didn't say a thing." Jim paused for a moment. "I just feel like my only part in this wedding is going to be as a guest. Bob is paying for the whole thing." Jim's tone always seemed to change when talking about his ex-wife's husband. "He just loves throwing his money around."

Hal jogged up the steps of the county building and waited at the top for Jim to catch up. "Julie loves you. You know that."

"Yeah." Jim seemed unconvinced.

"You're just bummed because you have a kid old enough to get married." Hal tried to lighten the mood. "Face it, you're catching up to me." He opened the door and held it for Jim.

"Hell, I'll never be that old." Jim grabbed the door and motioned for Hal to go through. "Age before beauty."

Hal and Jim took the elevator up to the third floor where the district attorney's office was located. Hal approached the receptionist. "We're here to see Arthur Jackson."

The woman looked up apathetically. "Do you have an appointment?"

"Yes." Hal smiled, though it was obviously insincere. "I'm Sergeant Lund, Salt Lake Police Department."

She picked up her phone and announced to the person on the other end that Sergeant Lund was there to see him. She hung up the phone and looked at Hal. "It'll be just a minute."

Hal and Jim walked over to the waiting area and each took a seat. "I told you," Hal said. "They think they're the most important people in the whole world. And to prove it, they make everybody wait."

Jim nodded in agreement. He picked up a *Sports Illustrated* and began thumbing through it. "Look at this guy." He held the magazine up in front of Hal. "He hits a little white ball around an oversized backyard and makes over three million dollars a year." He set the magazine back in his lap. "That's not a sport. Football's a sport. Basketball's a sport. I would even go so far as to say baseball's a sport, sort of, but golf is no sport."

Hal just smiled as Jim continued his ranting. He glanced at his watch. They had been waiting there for over ten minutes. Hal hated wasting time.

"He'll see you now." The woman announced. "His office is down this hall, last door on the left."

Hal and Jim followed the woman's directions to an office bearing Arthur Jackson's name. As they walked in, they were greeted by another receptionist. She smiled pleasantly. "You can go right in."

Arthur Jackson rose from his seat as Hal and Jim entered his office. "Sergeant," he said as he shook Hal's hand. "Detective," he greeted Jim. "This is my assistant, Greg Chadwick." The young man stood and shook hands with Hal and Jim. Jackson returned to his chair behind a large oak desk adorned with family pictures and expensive-looking figurines.

"Now, gentlemen, we need to go over all the evidence you've collected in the Harrison case. Was the suspect able to raise bail?"

"Yes, his family posted bond." Hal handed a large folder to Jackson. "This is what we have up to this point."

Jackson looked through the folder, taking his time. "So, we have established motive. Angry, possibly jealous husband with a bad temper and an unwanted divorce." He sat with a finger to his lips as if contemplating a deep question. "We have the murder weapon, which was

found in the suspect's possession. And we have a
suspect with an unsubstantiated alibi. Correct?"

Hal looked at Arthur Jackson. He smiled to himself, thinking this man could obviously afford a better
toupee. "We don't have anyone who can place him
anywhere else at the time of the murder." Hal paused
to clear his throat. "Mr. Harrison told us he was in
Vernal on business. However, we contacted the man he
was to meet with, and he said he called earlier in the
day to cancel the meeting and left town."

"Were there any other fingerprints on the murder
weapon?" Jackson asked.

"No, just Harrison's."

Arthur Jackson looked again through the file of
information Hal had given him. "You haven't established a crime scene?" He looked up at Hal.

"No. We haven't determined where the actual
murder took place," Hal answered. "Right now, we're
assuming she was murdered somewhere in Park City."

"And your search of her residence, what did it turn
up?"

"Well, we know that she went home after work
because the clothes she had worn to work that day were
on the bedroom floor." Hal continued, "She wasn't there
for very long, though. None of her neighbors saw her

that afternoon or evening, and she didn't bring the mail in from outside. The house seemed to be in order."

Jackson leaned back in his chair. "It said something in there about a tape from an answering machine?"

Hal looked over at Jim and nodded, wanting him to field the question. Jim cleared his throat. "Yes. We took the tape from her answering machine. There were only three messages. Her sister-in-law left one the day after her murder, and her supervisor at work called the following day. Her husband left a message the morning of the day she was murdered, apologizing for the night before. I believe there's a transcript of the messages in there," Jim said, referring to the file.

"The victim's mother says her daughter told her they had fought the night before," Hal added. "We assume that's what he was apologizing for."

"Have you got phone records?" Jackson asked.

"We've requested them, but we haven't received them yet. We pushed redial on Mrs. Harrison's phone and checked that number. The last call made from her home phone was to her mother." Jim looked to Hal for approval of the answer he had given. Hal nodded.

"No sign of struggle in the home?" Jackson tugged at his ear.

"No." Hal shook his head.

"Last person to see the victim alive, besides the suspect, was Nicole Wiscombe?" Jackson read the name from the file.

"Yes, she was a coworker of Mrs. Harrison's. She saw Mrs. Harrison get in her car in the parking lot after work." Hal shifted in his seat. "That was at quarter after four."

"No other suspects?"

"We have one other possible suspect at this point, but it's a real long shot. However, he left town in a big hurry after we first questioned him," Hal answered.

"And that's this Jeremy Kimball?" Jackson questioned.

"Yes. He has a prior record for assault. There is a lack of motive at this point, though, and finding the murder weapon in Mr. Harrison's truck has led us away from Kimball." Hal checked his watch. He was anxious to get out of Jackson's office and work on finding more leads in the case.

"Is there anything else?"

"We've impounded the suspect's truck and are checking it for traces of blood or hair from the victim," Hal said. "We're also working on locating the murder scene and hope to get evidence from that. We have a button and footprints found at the scene where the body was dumped, and we're working on matching those to the suspect."

"I'll go over this file in detail, and if I have any questions I'll get in touch with you." Jackson swiveled in his chair. "In the meantime, if you come up with any further evidence in the case, please contact me or my assistant immediately. We'll definitely be talking with you before the preliminary hearing."

Hal and Jim stood to leave. "We'll make sure you get everything you need," Hal said.

"What I need, Sergeant, is to have this case wrapped up in a nice, neat little package and delivered to my office." He met Hal's eyes with a fiery gaze. "I want a win on this one." Jackson leaned back in his chair. His face assumed an insidious smirk. "Of course, that shouldn't be too tough. I'd have more of a challenge beating an anorexic Jew in a pork-eating contest than I will annihilating that inexperienced little tramp in the courtroom."

Hal turned toward the door, biting his lip.

"Thank you, gentlemen," Jackson intoned, dismissing them. Greg Chadwick, who had listened silently to their discussion, smiled politely.

Jim and Hal walked to the elevator in silence. "What a prick!" Hal exclaimed as the elevator doors closed.

Jim laughed. "How do you really feel about him?"

"He's a pompous son-of-a-bitch." Hal's scowl slowly faded. "I'm half tempted to call animal control to come and snag that thing on his head." There was silence until the elevator stopped on the main floor. "Hey," Hal turned to Jim, "what do you say I buy you lunch?"

Jim looked at Hal in mock amazement. "You're going to buy me lunch?"

"You better take me up on the offer quick, before I change my mind."

"I'll never turn down a free meal." Jim grinned.

*   *   *

"Did you want to watch the news?" Jean asked as she entered the living room.

Hal sat in the dark, enjoying a cigarette. "No. I think I'll just go to bed. I've got to get up early and drive to Park City." Hal put his cigarette out in an ashtray.

"I wish you wouldn't smoke in here." Jean gave him a stern look.

Hal got up from his chair and stretched. "I know, hun. I'm sorry." He picked up the ashtray and carried it into the kitchen. "Should we go to bed?"

"Sure. I'll be there in a minute." Jean leaned over and received a kiss from her husband, then finished straightening the kitchen while Hal got ready for bed. It was about twenty minutes before she joined Hal in their bedroom. She fully expected him to be asleep, as was routine when he went to bed early. But Hal was lying in bed, wide-awake, staring at the ceiling when Jean entered the room.

Jean crawled into bed and pulled the covers up around her. "Having trouble falling to sleep?" She moved close to Hal and rested her arm across his chest.

"I just can't get this case out of my mind."

"The murder?" Jean asked.

"Yeah." Hal continued to stare at the ceiling as though its textured surface held the answers he was searching for. "It just doesn't make sense, and I think I'm the only one who feels that way."

There was a long silence. Jean gently ran her fingers over her husband's bare chest. "Do you want to talk about it?" she asked in a quiet voice.

Hal turned to his wife. "This woman who was murdered—supposedly she was on her way to Park City to get away for a few days. Her and her husband were separated and apparently not getting along too well. We find her car in a hotel parking lot in Park City and her body up Emigration Canyon. Her mother thinks the husband did it, because her daughter told her she was afraid of him and that they'd had a big fight." Hal paused for a moment before continuing. "There's a kid who works at the hotel where her car was found that has a criminal record and acted real nervous. Then we find the murder weapon in the husband's truck." Hal shook his head in dismay.

"So you don't think the husband is guilty?" From what Hal had said, his guilt seemed obvious to Jean.

Hal's gaze returned to the ceiling. "I don't know." He sighed. "It doesn't make sense. She was supposedly going to Park City. She told her mother that and had her pick up her son. But, there were no clothes or luggage in her car. She never checked into a hotel or even got reservations anywhere. Her death most likely occurred before witnesses testify her car was placed in the parking lot where we found it."

Jean went over the information in her mind. "But if they were getting a divorce, and he had the weapon in his . . ." She left her question unfinished.

"That's exactly what Jim and Merril say. And everybody else, for that matter."

"So what is it that's bothering you?" Jean asked.

"I just—I just don't want to make the same mistake I made before."

Jean was confused. "What do you mean?"

Hal turned to Jean. "The last murder case I had—the seventeen-year-old woman who was raped and stabbed—do you remember that?"

Jean searched her memory. "A couple of years ago?"

"Yeah."

"Yeah, I remember." She looked intently at her husband.

"The guy who was accused, Robert Archuleta—we had an eyewitness who identified him as the murderer, we had a fragile motive, and he had a criminal record. It seemed cut-and-dried." Hal paused for a long moment. "Halfway through the trial, another witness approached me, and through the information they gave me I uncovered some crucial evidence. Evidence that proved Archuleta's innocence." Hal's breathing accelerated. It was apparent that the subject carried with it a great deal of emotional stress. Jean lay beside Hal in silence, not knowing what to say.

Hal brought a hand up to rub his eyes. "I went to Davidson. He told me to hold off talking to the prosecution until he could look into it. Well, he just kept putting me off and putting me off. And I kept letting him. Two days before the trial was to end, Archuleta hung himself in his jail cell." He turned to Jean. "He was innocent. I had the information to prove it, and I did nothing." His eyes were pained.

Jean was shocked by Hal's revelation. "Why didn't you tell me?" Her question went unanswered. Hal's eyes closed, and he rubbed his face with both of his hands.

After a moment Hal spoke again. "I don't want to make that mistake again. I can't."

"But you did the right thing," Jean countered. "You went to your lieutenant and followed his instructions."

Hal released an unamused laugh. "Davidson was less than two years away from retirement. He didn't want to ruin a clean record with something like that, so he hung it on me." Hal's voice grew angry. "As far as my captain's concerned, it was me who withheld the evidence."

Jean was hurt that her husband had not shared something of such importance with her. "Hal, I thought we shared everything." She rolled away from Hal onto her back. "I had no idea."

"I was told I'd lose my job if I told anyone, including you. And besides, I didn't want to disappoint you." He sighed. "I'm sorry, honey. I'm sorry."

"I understand. I should have talked to you when I first found this lump, not after I went to the doctor. But I just—I didn't want to worry you." She rolled back on her side and put her arm tightly around Hal's torso. "Let's try and communicate a little better from now on. Both of us."

Jean's embrace caused Hal's heart to stir. He turned to his side and brought his face close to Jean's. "I have something else to tell you, then."

Jean was apprehensive. "What?'

Hal gazed into Jean's eyes for a long moment. "I'm scared, babe." His voice had become a whisper. "I'm scared to death."

"Of what? Of making mistakes? Hal, you're . . ."

Hal cut her comment short. "I'm scared to death of losing you."

Jean hesitated, hoping he would not sense her own fear. "You're not going to lose me." She reassured him, bringing a hand up to caress his face.

Hal took a deep breath and let it out slowly. "I have taken you so much for granted. And I've been so selfish." His jaw began to quiver. "I've become so selfish."

Jean watched this man—who was usually strong, trained to be unemotional and often detached—become childlike with fear, his chest heaving with emotion. She put her cheek to his and whispered softly in his ear, "I love you." She held him close, stroking his hair for a long while in silence.

Hal's breathing slowed. "You know, this whole thing about the new house—I guess a part of me thought if we made plans for the future and got involved in building a new house, then there was no way anything could happen to you." He laughed at himself. "I thought I could keep you immortal."

Jean smiled. "Honey, everything's going to be all right."

"You mean to tell me that you're not scared at all?"

"No, I'm scared, but I also have faith. I have to," Jean said. "I think the wondering is my biggest fear, you know? Not knowing." She paused. "I keep going over all these 'what-ifs' in my mind. What if it's cancer? What if I lose my breasts? What if it changes your feelings about me?" Jean struggled not to cry.

"My feelings aren't going to change, Jeanie. We'll fight this together. We'll fight it together." He brushed a tear from Jean's cheek.

"But what if they have to . . ."

"Hey," Hal interrupted her. "It doesn't matter." He put his hand in the middle of her chest, over her heart, and pressed lightly. "This is what matters." He stared down into Jean's gentle eyes. "I love you." He lowered his mouth onto hers and kissed her softly. His hand moved slowly across her chest and cupped her breast. His kisses grew more passionate as his fingers gently caressed her. Jean's body responded to Hal's familiar touch, rising to meet his flesh. He pulled away and tugged lightly on her nightgown. "You don't need this, do you?"

Jean quickly removed the garment and let it fall to the floor. Hal pulled her onto his chest, his desire inflamed by the feel of her warm skin against his. His fingers ran lightly over her back as their mouths eagerly meshed together. Hal's touch caused every nerve in Jean's body to tingle with excitement. She could feel his want, his need. It filled her with a calm self-confidence, replacing doubts and fear with renewed faith in their relationship, in herself.

Hal gently rolled Jean onto her back. He touched her cheek lightly and ran his fingers across her lips. "I love you," he whispered.

As their bodies merged again, he was overcome. Not with lust, but with a passion driven by the intense love he felt for his wife . . . and the ecstasy that came with bringing her pleasure.

CHAPTER 15

"The defense may call its first witness." The judge's voice seemed to reverberate across the silent courtroom. Jeni stood at the defense table staring into the sober face of the judge, his cold, apathetic eyes peering at her over the rims of his bifocals. She looked down at her client. Craig Harrison looked up at her, his deep brown eyes sparkling. He winked.

"The defense has no witnesses." She said. The faces of those seated in the jury box dropped in shock as they stared at Jeni incredulously. She felt her knees begin to shake and her stomach quiver.

"No witnesses?" The judge's voice boomed.

"No, sir." Jeni suddenly realized she could feel the carpet of the courtroom floor beneath her toes. She looked down, startled to find she had forgotten her shoes. She looked again at the jury, whose members began to whisper to each other. She turned to Craig, his warm eyes now filled with tears.

Jeni shot straight up in bed. Her hands were clammy, her face wet with perspiration. Her heart raced as she fought to control her erratic, heavy breathing. She felt as though a belt were strapped around her chest, slowly constricting. Her fingers tingled with pain, something she used to feel before debate competitions in high school and college. Her mind was frantic. She could feel her pulse, beating a rapid rhythm at her throat.

Finally, her respirations calmed. Jeni wiped the cold sweat from her palms onto the blanket that lay across her lap. She went to the bathroom and slowly drank a cold glass of water. "My God, I think I had an anxiety attack," she said aloud. Her haggard reflection stared back at her from the mirror. She tried to smooth her mussed hair, but with little luck. She noticed the sunken look of her eyes and leaned close to the mirror to exam them. Her recent inability to sleep well was taking its toll.

Upon returning to her bedroom, she glanced at the time. It was almost three a.m. Jeni went to the window and separated the vertical blinds, peering out at the city lights that stretched below. It looked quiet and peaceful, having a calming effect on her emotions. Her thoughts went back to the dream. What did it all mean? Was she totally unprepared to handle this case? Was it too much for her to handle? Did she need help? Was Craig Harrison really innocent?

The last question disturbed her. "This is not the time to be questioning these things," she said to herself. It was too late for that. She ran her fingers through her hair and returned to her bed. Laying her head on the pillow, she closed her eyes tightly. She went through a list of things, convincing herself of her competence and ability. Her anxiety eased as she thought of talking to her mother when her parents came for dinner. Her mother had always been a source of comfort.

"My parents!" She bolted upright again. She suddenly realized that they would be coming for dinner tonight. It had slipped her mind. She had worked a little on getting her house put together but still had a lot to do. The suffocating feelings of anxiety resurfaced. Would she have time? She would make time.

*   *   *

"Did you watch conference today?" Jeni's father asked as he took a second helping of spaghetti.

"Is conference this weekend?" Jeni asked.

"It's been the first weekend in October ever since I've been a member of the church." His answer was laced with sarcasm.

"Stan, Jeni's a grown woman with a very busy life. If she doesn't want to watch conference, that's her choice," Larae Sullivan intervened.

"Dad, things have just been so hectic lately . . ." Jeni tried to explain.

"It was a simple question, dear," he said to his wife. He gave Jeni a fatherly look. "Please pass the salt, Jen."

Jeni handed her father the salt, then turned to her mother. "How does Tom like living in St. George?"

"Oh, you know your brother, he can golf all year 'round now, so he's happy." Larae took another bite of her scorched garlic bread. "Did I mention that Mike got a promotion?"

"No!" Jeni beamed. "That's great! So what is he doing now?"

"Well, he's a supervisor in the maintenance department," her mother answered.

"He said he's basically doing the same job as before, but getting paid a lot more," her father added. He took a sip of his water and leaned back in his chair. "Are you dating anyone, honey?"

Jeni had dreaded this question that was inevitably asked every time she saw her father. "Well, Dad, not right now."

Larae got up from the table and began gathering dishes. "A lawyer who's running her own practice and just moving into a new house doesn't have much spare time for socializing." She gave her husband a you-know-better-than-to-ask-that-question look.

"Mom, sit down and relax. I'll get this." Jeni welcomed the opportunity to dodge the subject of her nonexistent love life. As she carried the plates into the kitchen, her thoughts went to Craig Harrison. She could picture him so clearly, his dark curls being gently tossed by a slight breeze, his eyes dancing as a quiet smile drifted across his lips.

"Jen?"

Jeni turned to find her mother standing next to her at the sink. "What?"

"Boy, you were a million miles away."

"I'm sorry," Jeni apologized. " I guess I've got a lot on my mind right now."

Larae looked around the kitchen. "I just love what you've done to this house. Your bedroom is beautiful, and I love the colors you've picked for this kitchen."

"Thanks, Mom." Jeni rinsed off the plates and began loading them into the dishwasher. "It'll be nice when I get everything just the way I want it, but I think it'll be awhile." She thought for a moment. "Do you think Dad likes it?"

"Oh, I think he loves it," she answered.

"He would love it a lot more if it came with a husband," Jeni muttered.

Larae took the glass Jeni was rinsing and set it down. She put her hands on Jeni's shoulders and looked into her deep blue eyes. "Honey, I'm so proud of you." She smiled. "You've done so well for yourself."

Jeni blushed. "Thanks, Mom."

"I just can't get over how independent and successful you are." She wrapped her arms around her daughter and gave her a big hug. "Just remember, Jen, your idea of success is the one that counts. It's not what I want for you or what your father wants for you; it's what you want for yourself."

"Thanks." Jeni greatly appreciated the support. She went back into the dining room and returned with another armload of dishes. Before long, they had everything cleaned up and put away. They joined Jeni's father in the living room where he was admiring her new furniture.

The rest of the evening went well. Jeni enjoyed catching up on the happenings in her family and chatting with her parents. There was only one more mere mention of Jeni finding a husband, and the comment was graciously intercepted by her mother.

"Good night. Drive carefully." Jeni shut the door and leaned against it. She felt much better about everything—her new house, her practice, even Craig Harrison's case—after talking with her parents, though she had not spoken about these subjects to them at all.

When she was younger, her mother had a rocking chair that was covered in a bright orange cloth. Jeni could remember many times sitting on her mother's lap and rocking. Her fears were calmed, her tears dried, her worries settled, her confidence boosted in that orange rocking chair. Though the chair had long since been discarded, and Jeni had long since grown up, her mother's soft voice and calming ways still had the same effects.

Jeni headed up the stairs to her office. She wanted to map out her plan of action regarding Craig's case and adjust her schedule accordingly. She stopped at her stereo system and put a Shawn Colvin disc in, then slipped behind her desk. Shawn serenaded Jeni while she worked, as the sun set over a bustling city.

CHAPTER 16

"I appreciate you seeing me, Sergeant Lund." Jenifer Sullivan smoothed her skirt before sitting on the chair Hal offered her.

"What is it that I can do for you, Ms. Sullivan?" Hal leaned back in his chair and looked at the attractive young attorney.

"Sergeant, I have some information that I think you might want to look into." Jeni pulled her briefcase onto her lap and opened it. She took out a sheet of paper and handed it to Hal. "This man, Darrell Lewis, was fired from Mr. Harrison's construction company on September sixteenth. When Mr. Harrison fired him, Lewis told him he would regret it. I looked up Lewis' criminal record and found him to be a familiar face at the county jail." Hal listened attentively as Jeni continued. "He has been convicted of four DUI's, one breaking and entering, two misdemeanor assaults, and one assault with a deadly weapon. I got his address and phone number from the construction company's records, but the phone has been disconnected. According to two of his neighbors, Darrell Lewis moved out of his apartment in the middle of the night without paying his rent, and they haven't seen him since." She paused. "He moved out on Thursday, September twenty-third."

Hal glanced again at the paper he held in his hand, then looked up at Jeni. "You believe your client is innocent, don't you?" His tone was matter-of-fact.

"Yes, I do." Her eyes were fiery, expressing conviction.

Hal toyed with his mustache. "Do you believe this man is involved?" he asked, referring to Darrell Lewis.

"I think it's a possibility, but I have very little information at this point." Jeni closed her briefcase and placed it on the floor beside her chair. "I would like to get a copy of the medical examiner's report and lab analysis, if I could."

"Didn't you get those from the district attorney's office?" Hal asked.

Jeni flashed an uneasy smile. "I worked with Mr. Jackson at the district attorney's office, and we had our differences. At this point he's being uncooperative."

Hal looked at her for a long moment. "Is there a reason why you think I will be more cooperative?"

Jeni returned Hal's steady gaze. "Because you're not convinced my client is guilty."

"What makes you say that, Ms. Sullivan?" Hal was intrigued by the attorney's remark.

"Because I believe it to be true. And if it's not, well, I guess I'm wasting my time then, and yours." Jeni's face was solemn and determined.

Hal rubbed his chin and looked down at his desk. He wondered if he should confirm what she apparently already knew. "I may not be completely convinced that your client is guilty, but I am definitely not convinced he's innocent." He looked again at Jeni. "We found the murder weapon in his possession. How do you explain that, Ms. Sullivan?"

"Mr. Harrison took that truck to Logan the day after his wife's murder. The truck was loaded with bricks. His toolbox and all of his construction tools were taken out of the truck and left in a storage shed at his office. He put the tools back in on Saturday when he returned to his office." Jeni reached for her briefcase again. "I just spoke with Mike Adamson, who works with Mr. Harrison." She pulled a notebook from her briefcase. "He helped Mr. Harrison sweep out his truck and put the tools back in on Saturday. He says he doesn't remember seeing the tire iron at that time."

"Is that all you have to go on? The word of your client, who's accused of murder, and a man whose livelihood depends on your client." Beneath his argumentative facade, Hal was impressed. Jeni was not only stunningly attractive but adept at doing her homework and committed to her job.

Jeni looked at the cluttered desk Hal sat behind as she pondered how to phrase her response. "Sergeant Lund, my client is a well-educated man who has successfully developed his own rapidly growing construction company. If," she emphasized the word, "if my client did kill his wife, why would he dump her body in a spot where construction was scheduled to begin six days later? Why would he not dispose of the weapon and choose to carry it openly in his vehicle? Why would he have deposited twelve hundred dollars into her checking account the day after she was murdered?"

Hal had asked himself those same questions. "Ms. Sullivan, in any homicide there are a lot of whys. And when someone is in the frame of mind to commit murder, they're not often going to follow that with rational behavior."

"But why, then, would my client have this?" Jeni
fished a small piece of paper out of her open briefcase.
"I got this from Mr. Harrison this morning."

Hal took the wrinkled piece of paper in his hand
and studied it. It was a receipt from an automatic teller
machine. The address of the ATM was 146 Dunmar
Street, Vernal, Utah. At the top of the receipt was
Craig Harrison's name and account number; the date,
September 21st, 1993; and the time, 6:12 p.m. Hal read
and reread the receipt for a sixty-dollar cash withdrawal.
His mind quickly went over the mileage between Salt
Lake City and Vernal. It was about a hundred and
seventy miles, which would mean roughly a three-hour
drive. That would put him back in Salt Lake City just
inside of the coroner's estimated time of death. But, it
was only a hundred and forty-seven miles from Vernal
to Park City, which would put him there well inside the
time range.

"You got this from your client this morning?" Hal
asked.

"Yes." Jeni cleared her throat. "When I spoke with
my client last week about his activities the day of his
wife's murder, he mentioned getting cash from the teller
machine. This weekend, as I was going over my notes,
the possibility of him having a receipt that showed the

time occurred to me. I called him last night, and he found it in his jacket pocket."

Hal did not know whether to be pleased with this new evidence or just further confused. "This doesn't guarantee his innocence. He could have been in Park City before his wife's death occurred."

"He had no idea his wife was planning a trip to Park City," Jeni countered.

"He *says* he had no idea his wife was going there," Hal emphasized. He sat for a moment staring again at the receipt. "Can I keep this receipt as evidence?"

"Yes, of course. I've made copies," Jeni answered.

Hal picked up his phone and pushed a couple of buttons. "Yeah, this is Lund. Could you send up a copy of the coroner's and lab reports?" He paused. "Thanks." Hal hung up the phone and looked at Jeni. "I'm still not convinced that Mr. Harrison didn't kill his wife, but it's my job to prove positive who did. I'm willing to work with the prosecution, and with you, in finding exactly who that is, Ms. Sullivan."

A man in a gray suit approached Hal's desk and handed him a folder. Hal quickly looked through it. "Thanks," he said as the man walked away. Hal glanced at his watch. He had a department meeting every Monday morning at ten, and he was about to be late. "If you'll excuse me, Ms. Sullivan, I have a meeting to get to." He stood up and offered his hand to Jeni. "Please, keep me informed of any other information you come across," he said as they shook hands.

"I will, Sergeant. And again, thank you for your time."

Hal handed the folder to Jeni. "Here are the reports you requested. I hope they'll be helpful."

As Jeni walked out of the detective division, Jim sauntered in. He turned to watch her shapely figure disappear down the hall. "Man, why do I always miss the good stuff?" he asked as he approached Hal's desk. "You ready for the powwow?" Jim's face was twisted into a toothy grin.

"What are you so happy about?" Hal asked as he donned his jacket.

"The boys came through yesterday! Did you watch it?" Jim's tone was enthusiastic.

"Football?"

"No, ballet," Jim said sarcastically. They walked together toward Lieutenant Bonner's office. "What did the babe want?" Jim asked.

"Advice on how to deal with offensive jerks like yourself," Hal said with a smirk.

"Yeah, right." Jim opened the door for his partner. "I taped the game if you want to see it. It was classic!" "Sounds good." Hal took a seat. As he waited for the meeting to begin, he contemplated the information Jenifer Sullivan had given him.

*   *   *

"There's no way this could have been counterfeited?" Hal looked at the woman across the counter from him who held the ATM receipt that bore Craig Harrison's name and account number.

"No, I don't believe so," the woman replied.

Jim walked into the bank and crossed the lobby to join Hal at the counter. "Here ya go." He handed Hal a receipt from the ATM that was located just outside of the bank's front doors. Hal placed it next to the receipt on the counter. They looked very similar. The bank's branch number and address were different, and James L. Webber's name and account number replaced Craig Harrison's. Other than that they were identical, including the thin, slick paper they were printed on.

"Thank you very much, ma'am. You've been very helpful." Hal nodded to the woman.

"You're welcome."

As they reached the front door of the bank, Hal turned to Jim. "Well, since you have sixty bucks burning a hole in your pocket, I guess you're buying lunch, huh?"

"Dream on, pal!" Jim struggled with the wrapper on a new roll of Lifesavers he had pulled from his pocket. "So now he has something to back up his alibi." He thought for a moment. "He could have given his card and pin number to somebody else, you know."

"That's redundant."

Jim looked confused. "What's redundant?"

"PIN number. PIN stands for personal identification number," Hal explained.

"Whatever." Jim shrugged his shoulders. "Think it's legit?"

Hal got in the car and lit a cigarette before answering. "They have surveillance cameras at ATMs, so that will be easy enough to verify." He took a long drag from his smoke and began backing out of the parking space. "It doesn't clear him, by any means, but it raises a lot of questions."

"Like?" Jim prompted Hal.

"Like her whereabouts from the time she left work until nine or so, when he could have caught up to her." Hal paused. "And the trip to Vernal . . ."

"Yeah. Why would he drive all the way there, turn around, go find his wife, and knock her off?" Jim looked to Hal in puzzlement.

"To establish an alibi," Hal said matter-of-factly.

"So, you think he did it?"

"Not necessarily. If he would have gone to all that trouble planning this thing, he would have been more careful with the murder weapon." Hal shook his head. "No, I'm still not convinced he's innocent, but I'm sure as hell going to be convinced of his guilt before I slack off on this investigation."

Jim thought for a long moment before speaking. "Maybe he didn't plan it. They had a fight Monday," he explained. "He looked her up on his way home Tuesday, the fight heated up again, and he killed her."

Hal looked at his partner. "Why are you so sure he's guilty?"

"He looks guilty. I mean, from the first time we talked to the guy, I thought he was guilty." Jim looked out the window at the passing cityscape. "We found the weapon on him, she was divorcing him—it just all fits together, and . . ." He paused.

"And what?" Hal badgered him.

"And my gut says he's guilty." Jim's tone was becoming defensive. "Why do you think he's not?"

"I said I wasn't ready to decide either way." Hal rolled down the window slightly and tossed his spent cigarette onto the road.

"Technically, you're breaking the law when you do that," Jim said.

"Do what?"

"Throw your butts out like that. That's littering. Two hundred and ninety-nine dollar fine." Jim grinned at his partner.

Hal shook his head. "I'm real sorry, Jim," he said mockingly, "would you like me to go back and pick it up?"

Jim ignored Hal's question and continued gazing out the window. "Ever been there?" he asked, pointing to the Triad Center.

"Yeah. Jean's sister was in charge of this big fund-raiser, and Jean dragged me there." A low chuckle escaped Hal's throat. "I've never seen so many anal-retentive people in one room in my entire life! I had to . . ."

Hal suddenly remembered why Helen Connor had seemed familiar to him. He had seen her at that fund-raiser. He strained his memory, trying to recall details about that evening three years ago. It seemed that Helen Connor was one of the bigwigs there.

"Earth to Hal."

"Huh?"

"You were saying?" Jim reminded Hal that he was in the middle of a story. "Oh, I don't remember," he answered. "Is this okay for lunch?" Hal pulled into Burger Town's parking lot. "Sure." Jim looked at Hal in confusion. "What's up with you?" "I just remembered seeing Helen Connor at that fund-raiser I was talking about." Hal got out of the car. "Go ahead and order for me. I've got to call Jean." He handed Jim a ten-dollar bill.

"Whaddya want?"

"I don't care, just a burger." Hal jogged over to a pay phone at the far corner of the parking lot. He took a quarter from his pocket and dialed his wife's office. After he got her on the line, he asked about the fund-raiser. "Hey, what's that arts thing that Merna's involved with?"

"The Salt Lake Valley Fine Arts Council?" Jean was puzzled by Hal's interest in her sister's civic affairs.

"Yeah. Is that the thing we went to the Triad for, a few years ago?"

"Yes. Why do you want to know about that?" Jean inquired.

"I just remembered seeing a woman there who's involved in the case I'm working on. Hey, could you give me Merna's number?" He remembered her recent surgery. "She's home from the hospital, isn't she?"

"Yes," Jean answered. "Her number is 555-7313."

"Thanks, hun. See you tonight." Hal hung up and dug in his pocket for another quarter. He called his sister-in-law and asked if he and his partner could stop by and ask her a few questions about the arts council.

*   *   *

"I thought about buying in this area when they first started building up here." Jim looked around the neighborhood he and Hal were driving through.

"Why didn't you?" Hal asked.

"I got such a good deal on the property out in West Valley. Of course, it was Granger back then. So we built out there. That was a nice little place, don't you think?" He looked at his partner.

"Yeah, I liked it."

"Beats the hell outa the shoe box I'm living in now," Jim spouted.

"Aahh, your place isn't that bad." Hal pulled into the driveway of a large brick home.

"Wow, nice yard!" Jim looked around at the neatly groomed landscaping.

"Bert is really into gardening." Hal commented. "Is that your brother-in-law?"

"Yeah. He's a pretty good guy." Hal stepped up to the door and rang the bell.

A slender woman with auburn hair answered the door. "Hi, Hal!"

"Hi, Mern." Hal leaned over and hugged her. "This is my partner, Jim Webber."

"Hi, Jim. It's nice to meet you."

"Ma'am." Jim noticed the woman's resemblance to Jean.

"Have a seat, and make yourselves comfortable. Can I get you anything?" Her voice was pleasant and upbeat.

"No, thanks." Hal took a seat on the couch, and Jim followed suit. "How have you been feeling? You look great," Hal added.

"I feel good as new." Merna took a seat in an overstuffed chair and pulled one leg up underneath her. "What can I do for you?"

"Do you know Helen Connor?" Hal asked.

"Yes. She's a permanent member on the arts board," Merna answered. "Why?"

"Elizabeth Harrison, Helen's daughter, was murdered a few weeks ago, and we're working on the case."

Hal opened his notebook. "What can you tell me about Mrs. Connor?"

"Oh, gosh, I don't know. She's one of higher-ups," she scratched the air with her fingers, indicating quotation marks, "you know, real wealthy, real showy. Most of the permanent members are."

"Is she divorced?" Hal questioned.

"No. Her husband died about five or six years ago. He owned RLC Construction. He died in an industrial accident, I think."

"RLC? That's one of the biggest construction companies in the state," Jim remarked. "No wonder she has so much money."

"Does she have any enemies that you know of? Anyone really envious or spiteful?" Hal looked to his sister-in-law for a reply.

"I don't really know. I know she's very well-known in the social arena. She's on just about every board and committee you can think of," Merna answered.

"So it's very possible that she has made some enemies." Hal paused. "You don't have an idea of anyone who harbors any bad feelings for her?"

"Not right offhand. She can be very opinionated and even condescending at times, but I think she's rather well-liked." Merna looked at Hal and shrugged her shoulders. "I don't really know. I'm sorry."

"That's okay." Hal got up from the couch.

"So, the woman who was found last week is Helen Connor's daughter? I didn't know she had a daughter." Merna walked Hal and Jim to the door. She leaned over close to Hal. "How's Jean?" she asked in a quiet voice.

Hal smiled at Merna. "Real good. Thanks, Merna."

"Where we goin' now?" Jim asked as they walked toward the car.

"Back to the station. We've got to make some phone calls and appointments, then we'll go from there."

"Give me the keys." Jim held his hand up as he walked around to the driver's side.

Hal tossed the keys to his partner, then clutched his chest with his hand. "Think this ticker can handle it? I'm getting older, you know." Hal smiled.

"Older and more of a pain in my ass!" Jim squeezed behind the wheel and started the engine.

"So Helen's husband owned RLC. I'm surprised Elizabeth didn't have a little more money," Hal said.

"I don't know. She seemed to have a lot of nice stuff."

"Yeah, but Craig's business seems to be doing well enough to afford that stuff. I mean, look at their house. RLC is a multimillion-dollar business. If she had even a portion of her father's money, she'd be living in a house three times that size, at least." Hal looked at his partner with a raised eyebrow.

"Guess so." Jim looked deep in thought as he drove. "RLC is still in business. Did she sell, or is she running it?"

"Good question. Guess that's one more thing for us to look into." Hal opened his notebook and jotted down a reminder for himself.

*   *   *

"Mind if I knock off a little early today?" Jim held the door for his partner as they entered the station.

"Naw, go ahead." A broad grin crept across Hal's face. "You got a date, big guy?"

Jim rolled his eyes. "I wish!"

"What's up?"

"I'm going over to talk to Arlene about the wedding," Jim answered.

Hal stopped in front of Blake Bartholomew's desk. "Hey, could you find out everything you can about RLC Construction for me?"

Blake looked up at Hal. "Anything in particular?"

"Find out who owns it, who's running it, financial situation, that kind of stuff." Hal waited for Blake's nod. "Thanks."

Hal removed his jacket and hung it over the back of his chair before sitting down. He leaned back and looked over at his partner. "This wedding thing is really botherin' you, isn't it?"

Jim settled his bulk onto his chair. "I just want Julie to know that I'm willing to do as much as Bob."

"You mean financially, or what?" Hal was a little confused.

Jim shook his head. "I don't know. I mean, I know Bob has tons more money than I do, but I could pay for this wedding." He stared down at his cluttered desk. "I just want to be a part of it, you know? I just want to be included."

"Does Arlene know you're coming over?" Hal asked.

"Yeah. I told her I'd be by sometime today." He looked up at Hal. "I feel like an outsider in my own family. I had a dream the other night that all the kids got married, and I missed all three weddings. When I woke up it was like, I don't know . . ."

Hal did not know what to say, so he reeled off the first thing that came to his mind. "Look, you can't change what's happened. You can't go back to the things you've missed, but you can change the way it's going to be in the future." He felt a little embarrassed offering such elementary advice.

"I know." Jim smiled.

Blake Bartholomew walked up and rested his slight frame on the corner of Hal's desk. "RLC is owned by Helen Connor and William Bradford. Bradford was an original partner in the business with Helen's husband, Robert Connor, but he got into some real financial trouble in '85 and Connor bought him out. Robert Connor died in '87 and Helen sold forty percent of the company back to Bradford. I'll have the financial information for you in the morning. Is that what you wanted?"

"Yeah, thanks."

"Sure." Blake started back to his own desk.

"Hey, could you check to see if Elizabeth Harrison owned any stock in the company?" Hal asked.

"Sure."

Jim waited for Blake Bartholomew to return to his desk before turning to Hal. "I bet it's the same Bill Bradford that's one of Arlene's neighbors. He's in the bishopric of her ward, I think." Jim stood and began gathering his things.

"Oh yeah?" Hal turned to his partner. "When you talk to Arlene today, would you mind asking about him?"

"No problem." He grabbed his keys from the top drawer of his desk. "Okay if I leave now?"

"Sure. Hey, I'll be off tomorrow and Wednesday. Jean's having some minor surgery."

"Everything okay?" Jim asked with concern.

"Yeah, fine. See ya Thursday." Hal watched his partner wave and walk away. "Good luck, buddy."

CHAPTER 17

Craig Harrison sat at the stoplight, growing impatient with the glaring red light. "C'mon!" he yelled as hit the steering wheel with the palm of his hand. The light finally changed, and Craig stomped on the accelerator. He pulled up to a parking meter in front of Jenifer Sullivan's office building. He bolted from his truck and hustled into the building without putting any money into the meter.

"I'm Craig Harrison. I called earlier." Craig looked to Kate Murdock for instruction.

"Yes, Mr. Harrison, have a seat. Ms. Sullivan is with a client but will be with you shortly." Her smile was pleasing and genuine.

Craig took a seat and picked a *Time* magazine up from the coffee table. He thumbed through quickly, not paying attention to the pages. He alternately looked to his watch and the door to Jeni's office. The moment the door opened, Craig was up and out of his chair. He watched as an elderly woman exited the room.

"Come right in," Jeni called to Craig from the door.

"They just went and picked up my son. The daycare center called me, but they were gone when I got there." He handed Jeni some papers. "This is what they gave me."

Jeni looked over the papers. The top one was notice of a custody hearing on October thirteenth, just a week away. The following paper was an order to place Ryan in state custody until the hearing. She quickly read through the order. She looked up at Craig, who remained standing next to her desk. "Your mother-in-law is seeking custody?"

"I guess so." Craig appeared agitated.

Jeni motioned for Craig to sit as she took a seat behind her desk. She read the order thoroughly. "So this was a complete surprise to you?"

"Yeah." Craig shook his head. "How can she do this? Is it legal?"

"Well, with the charges you have against you right now, yes. She's using that as leverage against you." Jeni looked puzzled for a moment. "Have you spoken with her?"

"No, not since I picked Ryan up last week."

"Tell me why you think she wants custody. Does she think you are guilty?" Jeni asked, though she was already under the impression that she did.

"Yes. But even if she didn't, I don't think she wants me raising her grandson. I'm not her favorite person."

"Why?"

"I don't know." Craig looked veritably riddled by the question. "She never cared for me or my family. Not from day one."

"What about Elizabeth's father?" Jeni leaned back in her chair and pressed her palms together.

"He was a pretty good guy. We got along all right. I worked for him for about five years. He hired me to work for his construction company when I graduated from high school." Craig bit his lower lip as he thought for a moment. "Two years later, when Liz and I got married, he made me a foreman and kind of took me under his wing. It was no secret that he wanted me to help him run the company when he'd retire. He told just about everybody."

"What happened then?" Jeni asked.

"He died in an accident on one of the construction sites. Helen owned the company then, and she fired me about a month after Robert died. He never put any of it writing, and she just fired me. Told me it was bad business to favor relatives." Craig ran his fingers over the black stubble that covered his stern jaw. "I took what I learned from him and started my own company. We struggled for a few years, but it's doin' pretty good now."

"But nothing ever happened to cause this animosity between you and Mrs. Connor?"

"Well, like I said, we never really hit it off, but when she fired me, I kind of laid into her about everything."

"Everything?"

"Just the way she was with Liz, you know, judgmental. Whatever Liz did, it just wasn't quite good enough. She's kind of a perfectionist." Craig seemed to be growing more nervous. "What are we going to do?"

Jeni felt overwhelmed with all that was happening. She could not imagine how Craig was handling it all. The empathy she felt for Craig suddenly tugged at her heart. "I'll do everything I can, but it's very unlikely that you'll be able to be with Ryan until after the hearing." She looked at Craig and felt the tingly excitement she experienced each time she saw him, even at moments as critical as this. "We'll get him back for you." She tried to catch the words before they came out, but could not. She hated making promises she was not sure she could keep.

*   *   *

"Can I help you?" the woman asked.

Jeni looked at the petite woman who sat behind the front desk at the business offices of RLC Construction, and she wondered how a woman with such an annoying, squeaky voice could get a job as a receptionist. "Yes, I'm here to see the manager, Mr. Bradford."

"And you are . . .?" The woman cocked her head to the side, something Jeni found annoying as well.

"Jenifer Sullivan."

"And you're here for . . .?" She looked at Jeni with wide eyes.

"I need to see Mr. Bradford. I called earlier this afternoon." Jeni smiled and wondered if the woman could see her true feelings through the forced gesture.

"Just a minute," she said to Jeni. The woman picked up her phone and spoke with someone, then directed Jeni down the hall to Bill Bradford's office. The door was open, and Jeni walked in.

A well-tanned man with prematurely white hair stood to greet her. "What can I do for you?"

"Mr. Bradford, my name is Jenifer Sullivan." Jeni gave the man a firm handshake. "I'm an attorney, and I'm doing some research for a case which involves the Connor family."

"Yes? And how can I help you?" The man sat behind a sizable desk with a solid marble top. It was impressive, but rather cold looking.

"Were you the manager when Craig Harrison was employed here?" Jeni was poised to take notes if needed.

"I was in management, yes."

"Are you acquainted with Mr. Harrison?" Jeni asked.

"Of course. He's Bob and Helen's son-in-law."

"Could you tell me what kind of a working relationship he and Mr. Connor had?"

"Well, Bob tried to help the kid out, you know. He gave him a job and moved him up. But Craig was kind of a cocky kid. Kind of a hothead."

Jeni was surprised to hear this about Craig. "What do you mean by 'hothead'?"

"Quick temper. He was a smooth talker, though." He leaned forward and rested his elbows on his desk. "Don't get me wrong. He wasn't a bad kid, just a little cocky. He grew out of it."

"Did Mr. Connor plan on turning the business over to him?"

The man broke out in laughter. "Are you serious?"

Jeni nodded.

"No."

"He never mentioned anything like that to you?"

"No, nothing. If he would have wanted Craig in management, Craig would be in management now." Mr. Bradford smiled, exposing a row of perfect white teeth.

"Do you know anything about Mrs. Connor firing him?" Jeni asked.

"I wasn't around when it happened, but I heard about it." He leaned back in his chair and raised his arms over his head, grasping the back of his neck. "Helen sent his pink slip down with the secretary. A few minutes later, Craig stormed into the office, and they had it out."

"Had it out?"

"He was yellin' at her, and she was yellin' at him. It got pretty ugly, from what I heard."

Jeni continued her questions. "Do you know why he was fired?"

"Helen was pretty tight-lipped about it. She didn't want to make Craig look bad. She said it had to do with

family." He seemed to enjoy gossiping about the past.
"Myself, I think he was skimming."

"Embezzling?" Jeni was surprised at the accusation.

"Yeah. Helen made a few comments that made me
think that, but she never came right out and said it or
anything." He sat up and tugged at his tie. "I don't
mean to be rude, Ms . . .?"

"Sullivan." Jeni helped him out.

". . . Ms. Sullivan, but I have a few things to take
care of before I leave, and it's getting a little late." He
stood and walked around to the front of his desk. "I
hope I helped."

"I appreciate your time, Mr. Bradford." Jeni walked
to her car, oblivious to the fact that Bill Bradford
watched her every step of the way, following her arous-
ingly feminine body as she walked out of the building
and across the parking lot.

Jeni drove down State Street through the tangle of
rush-hour traffic. It seemed that she was getting two
different pictures of Craig Harrison—one from him and
his family, and the other being painted by Bill Bradford.
She was troubled by the implication of impropriety on
Craig's part and the insinuation that he had a quick
temper.

After talking with Sergeant Lund, Jeni knew she needed more than the ATM receipt that placed Craig in Vernal the day Elizabeth was killed. What Lund had said about Craig being able to be in Park City before nine was true. But despite that fact and what she had just heard about her client, Jeni still believed in his innocence.

She had found some time before going to the construction office to read the reports Sergeant Lund had given her. What she had to do now was determine why Liz had decided on a spur-of-the-moment trip to Park City; why she hadn't mentioned it to anyone but her mother; and what had caused the abrasion on her forehead, leaving plywood splinters under her skin. If she could just answer those questions, Jeni thought, she could find the evidence to prove Craig was innocent.

In the meantime, Jeni needed to learn more about the woman whose life had been taken. The one person, besides Craig, who seemed to know Elizabeth best was Danielle. Jeni knew Danielle would be out of town until Friday and wondered how her curiosity might ease enough that she could wait four more days to speak with her. Thoughts of her unbearably busy schedule convinced her that Friday would be here before she knew it.

Chapter 18

A thin layer of smog hung over the south end of the Salt Lake Valley. Rays from the morning sun, which rose lazily above the peaks of the Wasatch Mountains, slowly dissipated the murky pollution. Hal glanced at his watch. Seven fifty-three. He looked again out the window. From the waiting-room on the fourth floor of Holy Cross Hospital, Hal could see most of the downtown area. He looked at the police station, nestled among a myriad of new highrises and a smattering of old buildings of historical and architectural integrity. The city Hal was sworn to protect was not without faults, but he would not live anywhere else.

The towering mountains that surrounded the valley, the majestic Great Salt Lake that bordered it to the north, and the salt flats and deserts that stretched westward all added to the unique beauty of Salt Lake

City. And, unlike in the majority of cities its size, people still knew most of their neighbors, and murder was something that still inspired shock and disbelief.

"Mr. Lund?"

Hal turned around to find a plump young woman wearing a blue hospital uniform standing behind him.

"Yes?"

"We need you to sign a few insurance forms." She handed a clipboard to Hal.

"We filled out paperwork when we got here this morning." Hal looked at the paper on the clipboard. The endless parade of forms he had seen all looked the same, and this one was no exception.

"We didn't get this form here." She pointed to the paper on the clipboard.

Hal looked up in bewilderment.

"Sign right there." The woman placed a pudgy finger on a line halfway down the page. Hal complied. "And right here on this one." She pulled the first page back and pointed to another line asking for a signature. When Hal had finished, she took the clipboard. "Thanks."

Hal walked over to a chair in the waiting area and sat down. More and more of the seats were being filled with people waiting for news of loved ones who were in surgery.

Hal picked up a magazine and began leafing through the pages. He glanced at the headlines and looked at the pictures, but his mind remained focused on his wife. He looked again at his watch. Eight-seventeen. Time had slowed to a snail's pace.

Jean had gone into the operating room just after seven. She had smiled as the gurney she rode on disappeared behind the swinging double doors that read "SURGERY." Hal liked to believe he was tough, hardened, strong; but he was just beginning to realize that Jean was his strength. He shook his head as he thought of his recent inner struggles. Why had it taken something like this to wake him up?

He tossed the news magazine back to the table and picked up a travel magazine. He found a feature article on the Virgin Islands. There were pictures of blue-green oceans, white-sand beaches and smiling tourists beneath green, leafy palm trees. Jean had always wanted to go on a cruise. Hal had held to the argument that a cruise was like being stuck in a crowded hotel with total strangers for an entire week. He was more for open spaces and natural wonders. And together, he and Jean and their children had seen a lot of them. Jean always gave in and did so with a smile.

The fear Hal had fought so hard to ignore came rushing to the surface. He could not imagine life without Jeanie, without her support, her patience, her acceptance, her warmth and understanding. Hal looked again at the pictures of the tropical paradise. At this point he would sell his very soul to share a moment on that beach with Jean, to know that she would be with him in the years to come. He was willing to spend the rest of his life floating endlessly on cruise ships, as long as that life included Jean.

Hal had faced many tense situations in his twenty-six years as a police officer. His life had been in danger, his career in jeopardy. He had spent hours in standoff situations with armed criminals, hours calming mothers whose children were missing, hours explaining to a young boy why his partner had shot his father. But the ensuing two hours were the longest, most grueling hours Hal had ever faced. They were spent waiting, wondering and praying.

*   *   *

"Dad?" Steve Lund walked up behind Hal.

"Hey, Steve." Hal's nervousness was visible to his son, something Steve had rarely seen.

"Have you heard anything yet?" Steve asked.

"No." Hal shook his head.

Steve walked around from behind the row of chairs and took a seat next to his father. "Chad and Trish should be getting here soon," Steve said, speaking of his younger siblings. "You doin' okay?"

"Yeah, fine." Hal tried to sound convincing.

"Mr. Lund?" A nurse in surgical garb called to Hal as she entered the waiting area.

Hal practically leapt from his chair. "Yes?"

The woman smiled. "Your wife is out of surgery now and is in the recovery room."

"How is she? How did it go?" Hal was desperate to know.

"She made it through the surgery really well. Everything went smoothly."

"Is she okay, though? Was it cancerous?" Hal's questions came rapidly.

"The doctor will be out in a little while to explain everything to you."

"When can I see her?"

The woman smiled politely. "As soon as she wakes up, we'll let you know."

Hal sat back down, relieved that the surgery was over, but still in the dark as to her condition. Steve put a hand on his shoulder and the two sat in silence, sharing each other's anxiety.

Trish and Chad arrived about twenty minutes after Hal had spoken to the nurse. Hal and his sons listened to Trish talk about her new experiences in college. Finally, Hal heard his name again. "Mr. Lund?" Another nurse came into the waiting room.

"Yes?"

"You can see your wife now." Her tone was matter-of-fact.

Hal walked toward the double doors, followed by three of his children. The nurse turned around, and seeing the four of them, she stopped. "You'll have to go in one at a time."

Chad gave his father a pat on the back, and he and his brother and sister remained in the waiting area.

Hal expected the nurse to take him to Jean. Instead, she led him to a small room just outside of the recovery area. "The doctor will be right out to get you," she said as she was leaving.

The next few minutes seemed like an eternity to Hal. Finally, the doors opened and the tall, gangly doctor approached. "How is she?" Hal asked, putting all formalities aside.

"Jean is just fine." The doctor's voice was deep and raspy. "Why don't you come with me, and I'll explain everything to you and Jean at the same time." He then led Hal through the doors and to a bed surrounded by drawn curtains. As he pulled back the curtains, Hal saw Jean. Her eyes drooped from the anesthetic, and her face was pale from the trauma, but a fragile smile graced her lips just the same.

"Hi, babe." He went to her side and grasped her hand. Bending down, he gently pressed his lips against her clammy forehead. "I love you."

Jean swallowed hard, and in a delicate voice she spoke. "I love you, too."

"Well, we got in there and found a lot more tissue than we anticipated," the doctor explained. "What we found were Fibroadenomas in both breasts. It's very rare in women over thirty."

Hal had no idea what the doctor was talking about. "Is it cancerous?"

"No." The word floated down to Hal like the song of an angel. "We removed the tissue to relieve the discomfort, but it was all benign." His face broke into a broad grin. "I'll leave you two alone." With that, he was gone.

Hal looked at his wife, who was squeezing his hand tightly. Her eyes sparkled beneath the tears that were forming. He reached down with his free hand and lightly brushed her cheek. "I knew you'd be all right," he lied.

"So, I guess we won't be building that new house after all." Jean managed a broader smile.

"Of course we will. That is, unless you've changed your mind." Hal caressed her face.

"Really?"

"As soon as I can get you out of here and feeling up to it, we'll go down to the realtor's and get things rolling." Hal leaned down and kissed Jean, then rested his cheek against hers. As he pulled away, Jean felt the moisture his eye had left. She looked up at her husband, deeply touched that he was strong enough to cry.

CHAPTER 19

"God, I love this place!" Hal took a deep breath of the mountain air as he stepped out of the Park City Police Station.

"It's too commercial," Jim muttered.

"It's no more commercial than Salt Lake. What's so commercial about it?" Hal asked.

"I don't know. It's just geared toward tourism."

"It's a tourist town, Jim. That's how they survive up here." Hal opened the car door. "People come from all over to ski the powder up here. Do you know how many celebrities own houses up at Deer Valley?"

"Like I care?" Jim got in the car.

Hal enjoyed the scenic drive through the streets of Park City. Even though tourists from around the world enjoyed skiing on slopes that were nothing short of breathtaking, the old mining town still had that rural, rustic feel.

"Well, that was a waste of time," Jim said as he watched the passing landscape. "I can't believe that we can't find one frickin' person up here that saw her."

"Such language! Hey, do you guys have a church committee that comes up with suitable substitutes for swear words?" Hal laughed at his own joke. "'Fetch'. 'Fetch' is my favorite."

"You're no cop. You're a regular comedian," Jim sneered.

"Although, 'dad-gum' is also a classic." Hal continued to mock his partner.

"You ought to be on Johnny Carson you're so funny!" Jim was not amused.

"It's Leno now." Hal reached into his pocket and pulled out a stick of gum. "Want one?" He offered Jim a piece of gum.

"Naw. You know, I don't . . ." Jim stopped in mid sentence. He looked at Hal with wide eyes. "Hey! You haven't had a cigarette all day!" Hal just smiled and continued chewing his gum. Jim looked at his watch. "It's one o'clock. You haven't had a cigarette since nine." His jaw was dropped in disbelief.

"I haven't had a cigarette since Tuesday."

"You're kidding me!" Jim slugged Hal in the arm. "Why didn't you tell me you quit?"

"You didn't ask."

"I'm proud of ya, partner."

"Thanks." Hal rubbed his arm.

Jim dug into his pants pocket and pulled out a wad of bills. "I've got twenty bucks says you don't make it past Friday."

Hal shook his head. "Thanks for the vote of confidence."

"I'm just kiddin'." Jim pointed out the window. "What are they buildin' there?"

"Probably more condominiums. Can you believe how fast this place is growing?" Hal looked out the window at the construction site. "Hey, did Arlene ever say anything about that Bradford guy?"

"Oh, yeah. It is the same guy. They live three houses down from Arlene, at the end of the cul-de-sac. She said she doesn't know him too well, but his wife, Carlene, is in the Relief Society presidency with her."

"That's a church thing, right?" Hal's tone was a little sarcastic.

Jim smiled. "You non-Mormons, you're so hard to train."

"Anything else?"

"Arlene says they've got kind of a holier-than-thou attitude, real showy. He's hardly ever home. His wife says he's a workaholic." Jim laughed. "He's had to have been home now and again; they have nine kids."

"Ouch! No wonder he had financial problems."

Jim looked out the window again. "So, if she was killed up here, do you think we'll ever find out where?" Jim asked.

"I don't know. I just think somebody would have seen something. Someone would have noticed her or her car. This thing's driving me nuts." Hal rubbed the back of his neck.

"You're already there, pal."

"Let's get some lunch and head back to the city."

*   *   *

Hal tossed his notebook and folder onto his desk as he walked past it to the soda machine. He returned to his desk and popped the top of a can of Pepsi as he took a seat. Thumbing through his messages, Hal stopped when he came to one from JoAnn Roselli. He got up and walked toward the doors. "I'm gonna run down to the crime lab and talk to Roselli. I'll be back in a minute," he said to Jim.

"Watch yourself. She's dangerous." Jim chuckled to himself.

Hal got an elevator key from the officer at the front desk and went to the lower level. "Roselli in?" he asked as he entered the lab.

"Room two," a man answered without looking up from his task.

Hal walked down the hall and found JoAnn Roselli starring into the eyepiece of a microscope. "Hey, I just got your message," he said.

The stocky woman looked up and rose from her stool. "I've got something for you." She walked over to a counter and opened a file. Inside were two photos of footprints that had been enlarged. "Your boot is a men's size nine and a half Red Wing. The man who wears them walks with his feet slightly outward and the outer edge of his boot is worn on the right foot. I'm guessing a stout man who favors his left leg slightly." She pulled a sheet of paper from beneath the photos. "There were traces of lime and mortar. Probably a construction worker." She placed the photos and paper back into the folder and handed it to Hal.

"No question on the size?" Hal asked.

"Definitely a nine and a half." She pushed her glasses up the slope of her nose. "Your button came from a heavy shirt or maybe a light jacket. We have two different colors of threads, brown and white. We're not sure yet on the type of material. I'll let you know as soon as we are."

"Thanks, JoAnn. You're the best."

"Tell Jarvis that," she said.

"I do, all the time." Hal smiled. "Thanks again."

Hal headed back up to his office, eager to find out what size shoe Craig Harrison wore. As he walked through the doors leading to his desk, he noticed Jenifer Sullivan sitting across from Jim. Jim looked up at him and rolled his eyes. He turned to Jeni. "That's the guy you'll want to talk to."

Jeni stood and followed Hal to his desk. "What can I do for you, Ms. Sullivan?" Hal asked.

"I just had a few questions about the coroner's report."

"Okay, have a seat." Hal offered Jeni a chair.

"Thank you." Jeni sat down and opened the notebook she had brought. "Your partner didn't want to cooperate with me."

"He gets that way sometimes. What can I help you with?"

Jeni skimmed over the coroner's report until she found the item she questioned. "Right here, it says there was an abrasion on Elizabeth Harrison's forehead, along with plywood splinters." She looked up at Hal. "Have you determined what caused this?"

"Well, being as we haven't established where the murder occurred, we're not sure. It could have happened while the body was being moved."

"But here," Jeni flipped the page and pointed toward the bottom, "the medical examiner lists postmortem injuries, and the abrasion isn't among them."

"Good point, Ms. Sullivan." Hal smoothed his mustache.

"Have you learned anything about Darrell Lewis?" Jeni asked.

"We tracked Mr. Lewis down to an alcohol rehab center in Boise. We won't be able to talk with him until we can get a court order and can make it up there." Hal picked up a pencil and began tapping it lightly on the edge of his desk. "Have you come up with any new information?"

"No. I thought I'd talk to as many people as I can over the next two days. I don't have any court appearances scheduled, so I'm going to take advantage of the time."

"Keep in touch."

"Thank you, Sergeant Lund." Jeni turned to leave.

"You don't happen to know what size shoe Craig Harrison wears, do you?"

"No, why?"

Hal shrugged his shoulders. "Just curious."

Jeni smiled and was on her way. Jim practically dislocated his neck watching Jeni walk out of the office. He got up and walked over to Hal's desk. "Man, if Bonner knew you were talking to her about the evidence we have, he'd have your hide."

"I'm going to tell you something, Jim." Hal leaned over the top of his desk closer to Jim. "Merril Bonner can kiss my ass if he can jump that high."

CHAPTER 20

The autumn air was crisp and cool, and a light breeze tossed the last of the fallen leaves about. Jeni walked down a street lined with barren trees. Towering maples, which in the summer provided bountiful shade, looked naked and exposed with not a leaf clinging to their branches.

She paused in front of the house just west of Elizabeth Harrison's. Jeni had spoken with eight people in the neighborhood, finding nothing that Sergeant Lund had not already told her. She walked up the steps of the porch and was about to ring the bell when she noticed a woman and a young boy raking leaves to the side of the house.

"Excuse me?"

The woman turned. "Yes?"

"Hi, my name is Jenifer Sullivan. I'm an attorney. I was representing Elizabeth Harrison in her divorce before she was killed, and I was wondering if I could talk with you for a minute."

"Sure." The woman leaned her rake against the house and removed her gardening gloves. "I'm Nancy Clements." She offered her hand in greeting. "This is my son Jared."

"Hi, Jared." Jeni smiled at the blond-haired boy, who nodded.

"Were you very close to Elizabeth?" Jeni asked Mrs. Clements.

"Mmm, not really. We talked now and then. I have a son that's just a year older than her son, Ryan, and they played together quite a bit."

"A detective with the police department told me that someone at this home saw Craig Harrison's truck at Elizabeth's house the day she was killed. Was that you?"

"Yeah. I was carrying groceries in from the car, oh, sometime around four-thirty, quarter to five, and I saw his truck pull into the driveway there." She shrugged her shoulders. "I didn't really pay any attention, though."

"But you're sure it was his truck?"

"Yeah, it was a big truck. Ford, I think. Dark, either blue or black, and it had a construction company's name on the doors." The woman tucked her hair behind her ears.

"Mom," the boy who had been quietly listening spoke up. "Mr. Harrison's truck is brown."

"Well, it was a dark color," the woman said.

"No. You're talking about the other truck that was there a couple of times."

The woman looked at her son. Jeni questioned him, "When did you see the truck?"

"Week before last," the boy replied. "I was just getting home from delivering papers, and I saw a man pull the garage door up and pull his truck in. He left a few minutes later. He came by again a couple of days after that."

"What time do you get back from delivering the paper?" Jeni asked.

"Around five, usually."

"He delivers the *Deseret News*," his mother added.

"Do you know what day it was?" Jeni was hoping he could remember.

"Either Monday or Tuesday." He hesitated. "Could have been Wednesday, I guess. I just remember that I got home from school a little later than usual. I had inserts in the paper, so I really had to hustle."

"Do you remember the company name on the side of the truck?"

"No." Jared shook his head. "Sorry."

"What did the man driving look like?" Jeni asked.

The boy shook his head. "I don't remember."

"But you're sure it wasn't Mr. Harrison?"

"Pretty sure."

"Thanks," Jeni said. "You've been very helpful. Do you mind if I tell the detective and have him get in touch with you?"

"That's fine," Mrs. Clements answered.

Jeni walked back to her car and looked in her notebook to find the next stop on her list.

*   *   *

Parking places were scarce in front of the Little Willow Daycare Center. Jeni finally found one around the corner and walked the half block to the preschool.

"Can I speak with Lisa Bowen?" Jeni asked the woman who approached her.

"I'm Lisa. What can I do for you?" the young woman asked cheerfully.

Jeni introduced herself and explained why she was there. "How many times a week did the Harrisons bring Ryan here?" she asked.

"Usually four, sometimes only three. It depended on Mrs. Harrison's work schedule."

"Was she ever late picking him up, or did she change her plans frequently?" Jeni was a little distracted by the noisy children.

"No, not that I can think of."

"How well do you know Mrs. Harrison's mother?" Jeni inquired.

"I met her a couple of times is all. She seemed very nice, very polite." Lisa bent down to answer a little girl's question, then sent the toddler to play with the others.

"So it wasn't unusual for Mrs. Harrison to have her mother pick Ryan up?"

"Well, twice before she had called and told me her mother would be coming by to get Ryan. Usually it was because she'd be working late, and her husband was working, also."

"Did she call you the last time?" Jeni waited for an answer.

"No. No, she didn't." She shook her head.

"But each time before, she called to inform you that her mother was coming and not her?"

"Yes. In fact, she had her sister-in-law come and get him a couple of times, too, and she called those times, also."

"Thank you. I'm sorry to have taken you away from your work."

"No problem." She smiled. "Have a good day."

Jeni went over all of the things she now knew about the case as she drove from the daycare center to the mall. She tried to piece things together in an order that made sense. Why hadn't Elizabeth called the daycare center when she called her mother? So many questions went through Jeni's mind. Her belief in Craig Harrison's innocence remained solid. What troubled her now was the lack of a viable suspect other than Craig. Darrell Lewis was indeed a man with a track record; but also, as his record showed, a man of impulse, not one to map out an intricate plan.

The police report had named Jeremy Kimball as a possible suspect prior to the discovery of the murder weapon and Craig Harrison's arrest. Again, there was lack of a plausible motive and a criminal record that indicated impulsive outbursts of violence directed not at strangers, but at family members and friends.

Before she knew it, Jeni had arrived at the Fashion Place Mall. She turned into the parking lot and found a space close to Feldman's south entrance. She walked past the shoe department to the jewelry counter and asked the clerk for directions to Sarah Hepworth's office.

"Just take the escalators up to the third floor, and then go all the way to your right." The woman's lips curved upward into a pleasing smile. "You can't miss it," she added.

"Thank you." Jeni found her way to the escalator and watched the first floor grow smaller and smaller below her as she rode upward. When she reached the second floor, she turned and rode a second escalator to the third floor. A sign directed Jeni to the business office.

"Hello. I'm looking for Sarah Hepworth." Jeni spoke to the woman at the reception desk.

"I'm sorry. She's on vacation until next Thursday," the woman answered. "Is there someone else that can help you?"

"My name is Jenifer Sullivan. I'm an attorney for Elizabeth Harrison's family, and I wanted to get some information about her employment here," Jeni explained.

"I see." The woman seemed flustered upon hearing Elizabeth's name.

"Ms. Sullivan, maybe I can help you." A red-haired woman arose from her desk and approached Jeni. "I'm Jan Francom, public relations." The petite woman's perfume was almost overwhelming. "Why don't we go into the break room." She motioned to the door across the hall.

Jeni was led into a room crowded with tables and chairs. One wall was lined with vending machines, the other three adorned with pictures of past employees of the month. Elizabeth Harrison's smiling face caught Jeni's eye.

"She was great with the customers." Jan Francom joined Jeni in admiring Elizabeth's plaque and picture. "Even if she was in a bad mood, she never took it out to the floor with her, you know? Always smiling and polite when it counted."

Jeni turned to Ms. Francom. "Was she in a bad mood often?"

"No. Quiet, maybe, but not what I would call a bad mood." The woman motioned Jeni toward a chair. "Now, what can I do for you, Ms.—Sullivan was it?"

"Yes." Jeni took a seat in one of the plastic orange chairs that surrounded the tables. "What I'd really like to do is get a feel for the state of mind Mrs. Harrison was in, the day she was murdered." Jeni paused. "Is there anyone here she confided in about her personal life? Did she have close friends here?"

"Well, she was friendly with just about everyone. As far as close friends go, I wouldn't know. I do know, however, that the police detectives have talked to just about every employee here, so I'm sure if there was any helpful evidence they'd have discovered it."

Jeni could not decide if the woman's courteousness was genuine or contrived. "Yes, I realize that they have talked with several employees. I just can't help but feel that somewhere they've missed something." Jeni was having a hard time expressing her questioning feeling with words.

Ms. Francom looked at Jeni, her eyes narrowing slightly, as if she were sizing her up. "Are you the attorney defending her husband?"

"Yes, I am."

"I think you'll probably want to talk with Sarah when she gets back from vacation." The woman rose from her chair. "I'm sorry I couldn't be of more help."

Jeni followed Jan Francom out of the breakroom.

"Good day, Ms. Sullivan." She remained polite to the end.

Jeni just smiled and nodded. She walked out toward the escalators and had almost reached them when the receptionist came running after her.

"Excuse me," she said, offering a Feldman's bag to Jeni.

"Yes?"

"I cleaned out Liz's locker last week, and I wasn't quite sure what to do with her stuff." She handed the bag to Jeni. "I guess you'd be the right person to give it to."

Jeni opened the bag. There was a Sony Walkman, a couple of cassette tapes, a notebook, three dollar bills and some make-up. "Thank you. I'll see that it gets to her family."

* * *

"Hi, Kate," she greeted her secretary as she hustled through the door.

"Jeni, your two-thirty canceled." Kate did not look up from her typing. "Did you get some lunch?"

"Not yet," Jeni said as she walked into her office.

"What am I going to do with you?" Kate mumbled in a caring voice.

Jeni emptied the contents of the Feldman's bag onto her desk. She picked up the cassette tapes. One was Melissa Etheridge's "Brave and Crazy" and the other was Heart's "Little Queen."

She opened the notebook and flipped through the pages. There were grocery lists, to-do lists and a number of half-finished poems. Jeni began reading a poem on one of the first pages. It was entitled "Life Sentence."

> *I thought these feelings would go away,*
> *like so many dreams that fade and die.*
> *I offered my heart, my soul, my ten percent to God*
> *with one simple request—*
> *that I feel for him what I have felt for you.*
> *But this emptiness remains,*
> *this wanting, this desire.*
> *How long will my heart be imprisoned?*

Jeni lifted the receiver of her phone and rang Kate's desk. "Hold my calls for now, would you? Thanks."

As she flipped through the pages, she read the fragments of poems. She read notes Elizabeth had written to herself, reminders of important appointments, and such. Toward the middle of the notebook was a page with Jeni's name on the top and a reminder of the appointment she had set up for her and Craig to meet with Jeni. Elizabeth had made that appointment the day before she was killed. Below that was a paragraph of writing, almost like a journal entry.

I can't believe that I told her. She pushed me into it with her questions. Now that she knows, I'm sure I'll be disinherited. That's a laugh. Danielle warned me not to tell my mother I don't know how many times. Why didn't I listen. I'm afraid to tell Dani. I wonder what she'll do when she finds out. Hopefully she won't. I can't believe that Mom figured out that it was Dani I had been with. Dani is going to freak! What have I gotten myself into?

Jeni leaned back in her chair, contemplating what she had just read. Was Elizabeth having an affair with Craig's sister? Jeni shook her head and leaned over her desk to again read the words. She looked through the pages that followed, but other than a shopping list on the next page, this was the last entry.

She was overwhelmed with the implications of what she had read. Her next thought was of Craig. Did he know? He and Danielle seemed to be so close. He could not possibly know; it would kill him. Her thoughts went to Danielle. Was Elizabeth afraid of her? Had Danielle found out? Jeni's mind was swimming with the possibilities.

CHAPTER 21

Jim carried two white paper sacks into the detective division while balancing a briefcase from the fingers of his other hand. He walked to Hal's desk and deposited one of the bags. "Turkey, right?"

"Yeah. Did you get extra mustard?" Hal opened the bag and pulled out a sandwich and some chips.

"Yeah." Jim lumbered back to his desk and pulled his lunch from the other bag.

"Hal, could I see you for a minute?" Merril Bonner called from the doorway to his office.

Hal got up from his desk and hustled to his lieutenant's office. "What is it?"

"I need you to take this burglary in the Avenues." He handed Hal a report.

"Okay." Hal looked over the report and started to leave.

"Hal, could you close the door for a sec?"

Hal looked up at Bonner and closed the door.

"You're spending entirely too much time on this Harrison case. We have our man, and you have plenty of time before it goes to trial to do your follow-up work. I need you clearing up some of these other cases."

Hal had sensed this coming for a while. "Lieutenant, I've found some evidence that suggests that we might not have our man. It's my job to secure a solid case against a suspect, and we just don't have that at this point," Hal argued.

"Hal, we have the murder weapon, fingerprints, motive. What more do you need, for Chrissake?" Bonner's temper began to flare.

Hal took a deep breath. "It's not that cut and dried."

"Look, everybody here knows what happened with Archuleta, and we all feel bad about it, but you can't let it cloud your judgment on every case you come up against." Merril Bonner rubbed his chin. "Let it go."

Hal held his tongue, though it was a difficult task. "Is that all?" he asked.

"Yeah, that's all."

Hal walked back to his desk, his anger rising with every step. His face was flushed, his jaw clenched.

"Hey, slick, you got a call on line one," Jim called to his partner.

Hal picked up the phone. "Sergeant Lund."

"Sergeant Lund, this is Jenifer Sullivan. I have some information I'd like to share with you. Is there a time I could meet with you today?"

Hal looked over his shoulder at Merril Bonner's office. "I'm going to be leaving here shortly to investigate a burglary. How important is this information?"

"I think it's crucial," Jeni said.

"Can you tell me about it now?"

"Well, it's kind of hard to explain on the phone."

Hal thought for a minute. "Will you be in your office later this afternoon?"

"Yes."

"Why don't you give me that address, and I'll stop by on my way back to the station."

Jeni gave Hal the address and reiterated the importance of the information she had for him.

"Eat fast, would ya?" Hal said to Jim. "We've got a 10-91."

Hal picked up the sandwich he had only tasted and tossed it into the wastebasket next to his desk. He had left his appetite in Lieutenant Bonner's office.

*   *   *

"Man! Can you believe that guy?" Jim tugged uncomfortably at his collar as he and Hal walked down the driveway to their Corsica. "Talk about insurance fraud." He looked up at the overcast sky. "Think it'll rain?"

Hal looked around him. "Looks like it." As he got in the car he laughed and shook his head. "He should have at least broken the window from the outside to make it look good."

"So how do we handle this one?" Jim asked.

Hal looked behind him as he backed up. "We write up the report, turn it in, and let his insurance company deal with the headaches."

"Serious?"

"It would take too much of our time to try and prove that it's a crock. That's what insurance investigators are for."

Jim informed dispatch that they were en route to the station.

"We have one stop to make," Hal informed him.

"Where?"

"Jenifer Sullivan's office." Hal drove down South Temple and turned south onto Fourth East.

"You got a thing for her?" Jim raised his eyebrows.

Hal answered with a contemptuous look.

"You know you're askin' for trouble," Jim said.

"I'm just doing my job. She called and said she had some information she thought we should be aware of." Hal pulled up to the office building at 448 South. He led the way down a flight of stairs to Suite B, where a placard hung that read "Jenifer Sullivan, Attorney at Law."

"Can I help you?" the middle-aged woman behind the reception desk asked.

"I'm Sergeant Lund, and this is Officer Webber. We're here to see Ms. Sullivan," Hal announced.

"Okay, I'll let her know." Kate got up from her desk and entered the office behind her. A moment later she emerged and motioned for Hal and Jim to enter.

Jeni met them in the middle of the room with an eager handshake. "I appreciate you coming down." She gestured toward a long couch. "Please, have a seat." She picked a blue spiral notebook up from her desk and took a seat in the chair next to Hal. "A woman from Feldman's office gave these items to me." Jeni pointed to the articles atop her desk. "They were taken from

Elizabeth Harrison's locker." She held up the notebook.
"This was among those belongings. It has shopping lists,
to-do lists, a few attempts at poetry, and what you might
consider random journal-type entries." Jeni handed the
book to Hal.

"They really should have given them to us." Jim
seemed annoyed.

"It was a young girl. She probably wasn't thinking,"
Jeni speculated.

Hal opened the notebook and paged through it.
"Why is this significant?" he asked.

"If you'll turn to that marker . . . " Jeni pointed to a
small piece of paper that protruded from the top of the
notebook toward the middle.

Hal complied and began reading from the page.
After a moment he looked up at Jeni. "Was she having
an affair?"

"That's what it leads me to believe." Jeni motioned
toward the notebook. "There's some poetry in there that
suggests the same thing."

Hal thumbed through the pages, scanning the words.
"Have you discussed this with your client?"

"No. I didn't know how to approach him with it."

Hal looked intently at Jeni. "Do you think he found
out about it?"

"No." Jeni shook her head.

"What's your theory?" Hal asked as Jim read over his shoulder.

"I'm not sure. That's why I called you. I didn't know what to think," Jeni replied honestly.

"Do you think Danielle Harrison is a possible suspect?" Hal raised his eyebrows.

"I wouldn't dare rule her out at this point."

"Have you talked to her?" Hal inquired.

"No. She's out of town on business."

"Do you know when she'll be back?"

Jeni cleared her throat. "She's due back tomorrow afternoon."

Hal made a note of that. "Have you talked with Mrs. Connor?"

"No. I wanted to talk to you before I discussed the matter with anyone," Jeni answered.

"We appreciate that, Ms. Sullivan. Officer Webber and I will pay her a visit and see if she knows something that might help us." Hal stood. "Thank you, Ms. Sullivan. Do you mind if we take this with us?"

"That's fine." Jeni walked them to the outer office and said goodbye.

Jim and Hal walked to their car in silence. After Hal pulled away from the curb, Jim piped up. "So, she was a dyke." He shook his head in disgust. "No wonder he killed her." The remark garnered no reply from Hal. "Boy, who would of thought it of a goodlookin' babe like that, though? She didn't look like no football player."

Hal rolled his eyes at his partner's ignorance.

"Some defense attorney, bringing us evidence against her client," Jim continued.

"What makes you think it's evidence against him?" Hal asked.

"Are you kiddin' me? You don't think that spells out why he knocked her off?" Jim popped a Tic Tac in his mouth. "Myself, I don't blame him. I mean, it's bad enough when your wife leaves you for another man, but for another woman! That's the lowest. And his own sister!" He shook his head.

Hal turned to his ranting partner. "Jim, what would you do if one of your kids came to you one day and told you they were gay?"

"I'd kick their ass and send 'em to a shrink."

Hal shook his head.

"Why, what would you do? Just accept it?" Jim's demeanor was growing indignant.

"I have a brother who's gay." Hal looked at his partner with piercing, angry eyes. "It's people with attitudes like yours that make his life a living hell."

There was a long silence between them as they drove toward the east bench of the Salt Lake Valley. Jim's gaze remained focused out the passenger side window. Finally, he spoke. "Hey, I'm sorry, Hal. I didn't know."

"Just forget it, would ya?" Hal pulled up to Helen Connor's house and shut off the engine.

Helen came to the door, surprised to see the two officers. "What can I do for you?"

"We'd like to talk to you for a minute, if you don't mind," Hal answered for both of them.

"Yes, come in." Helen led them to the posh room where they had interviewed her before. Hal was impressed with how immaculate it appeared.

Hal and Jim took a seat on the couch across from the silver-haired woman. "Ma'am," Hal began, "we've been given some information about your daughter that we understand you were made aware of just before her death."

Helen narrowed her eyes and cocked her head to the side. "What are you talking about?"

"Was your daughter having an affair with her sister-in-law?" Hal's question was direct.

Her jaw clenched. "That's absurd!" Her tone was curt.

"Did your daughter ever approach you with that information or discuss homosexual tendencies with you?" Hal's eyes remained locked on Helen's face, watching her reaction.

Helen's eyes narrowed. "No. Where did you get this information? Obviously someone's trying to slander her name. For what reason, I don't know." Helen's spoke with a bitterness. "It's a lie, an unadulterated lie."

"So your daughter never said anything to you about having an affair with her husband's sister?" Hal asked, clarifying Helen's answer.

"No! It's all a lie!" she exclaimed, fighting for composure. She got up from her chair. "Now, if you gentlemen don't mind, I have better things to do than to sit and listen to disgusting untruths about Elizabeth." Her eyes were fiery.

"We don't mean to upset you, ma'am. We're just trying to get to the truth." Hal remained seated.

"The truth? It seems you people want everything but that." Her voice was biting and acrid. "You had the man who killed her in jail, but he's out walking the streets, free, and you're wasting your time barging into my home and spouting untrue vulgarities about my daughter. Now," she said calmly, "if you don't mind, I have other business to attend to."

Hal stood up and ran his tongue over his upper lip as he thought. "Mrs. Connor, if your daughter had said something of that nature to you, how you would have reacted?"

Helen shot a vexing glance at Hal. "Good day, officers." She remained standing next to her chair.

"Hey babe, could you . . ." A man walked into the room and stopped, startled by the presence of visitors.

Helen smiled uncomfortably. "Bill, this is Detective Lund and Detective Webber." She gestured toward Hal and Jim respectively. "This is Bill Bradford, my business partner." The man nodded. "I have business to discuss, gentlemen. I trust you can see yourselves out."

Jim stood, waiting for Hal to move. Hal lingered next to the couch. "Mrs. Connor, if you happen to remember any conversations you had with your daughter regarding this, I'd appreciate it if you'd contact us." Seeing no response from Helen, Hal started toward the door. After taking a few steps, he stopped and turned back. "Mrs. Connor, you were home the night your daughter was killed, weren't you?"

"I was here with my grandson all night the night she was murdered. The Ladies Auxiliary officers had a dinner meeting here from six until after ten o'clock." The words were thrown at Hal as if they were weapons.

"I was simply clarifying, ma'am."

"You have no right to stay here. You have no warrant." She turned and walked toward the door. "If you don't leave, I'll have to file a complaint."

Hal looked at Jim who shrugged his shoulders. They walked out without saying another word to Helen.

"Did he call her 'babe'?" Jim asked as they got in their car and turned around.

"That's what I thought he called her." Hal shook his head. "Maybe he's not a workaholic after all, huh?"

CHAPTER 22

Jeni pulled up to 647 Gloucester Avenue, the address Danielle Harrison had given as her home. She turned off the car's engine and sat for a moment, gathering what little courage she could muster. This was a situation she was not sure how to handle. Jeni took a deep breath and made her way to the door.

"Hello." Robin Curtis seemed surprised by Jeni's visit.

"Hi, I'm here to see Danielle."

"She hasn't made it home yet, but I expect her any minute. Would you like to come in?"

"Thank you." Jeni walked into a living room nicely decorated in earth-tone colors.

Robin gestured to a sofa. "Have a seat. Can I get you anything? I just finished brewing some iced tea."

"That would be great. Thanks." Jeni felt awkward and uncomfortable, having only met Robin Curtis briefly before. She looked around the room at the decor, trying to get more of a feel for Robin and Danielle's personalities.

"Do you prefer sugar or saccharine?" Robin stuck her head around the corner from the kitchen.

"Saccharine, thanks."

A moment later, Robin returned with two tall glasses of iced tea. "I'm addicted to this stuff."

"Thank you." Jeni took a sip from her glass. "Mmm. That's really good."

There was a moment of uncomfortable silence before Robin spoke again. "How are things looking for Craig?"

"We're hopeful." Jeni took a long drink of iced tea. "I see you're a Nagel fan," Jeni said, referring to the artwork that adorned the walls.

"Yeah, you too?"

"I like his work."

"He kinda had to grow on me." Robin gulped down a good deal of her tea. "When we bought the house, Dani insisted on the Nagels. And, obviously, she usually gets what she wants." Robin smiled.

"How long have you lived here?"

"Let's see, we bought it in March of '91, so two and a half years now."

"Do you like the area?" Jeni asked.

"It has its pros and cons. Most of our neighbors keep to themselves." A car pulled up outside, and Robin looked out the window. "Dani's home." She got up from her chair. "I'll go help her with her luggage."

Jeni grew nervous. She still had no idea how she was going to approach the subject of Danielle's relationship with Elizabeth. She looked up to see Danielle walking through the door with a travel bag slung over her shoulder.

"Hi. How are you?" Danielle offered a tired smile.

Jeni stood and smoothed her dress. "Hi. Good. I'm sorry to bother you, but there are a few things I'd like to discuss with you, if you have a few minutes."

"Sure. Let me just throw this stuff in the bedroom, and I'll be right back." Danielle walked past Jeni and down the hall, followed closely by Robin. A moment later she emerged. "So, what can I do for you?"

"I'm sorry to bother you. I know you're just getting back from your trip, but I've discovered something that could be crucial to this case."

"It's no problem." Danielle turned to Robin, giving her a signal with her expression.

"I'll be in the other room unpacking your bags, if you need anything." Robin gave Danielle's arm a gentle squeeze.

"Okay." Danielle walked to the chair across from Jeni and sat down with a heavy sigh. "I hope it's good news."

"I'm going to get right to the point. I don't want to offend you, and I apologize for asking a question of such a personal nature. But I have to know the whole situation surrounding Craig and Elizabeth's divorce." Jeni stopped to swallow and take in a slow, deep breath. "Were you romantically involved with Elizabeth?"

Danielle was taken aback by the question. "Did Craig tell you that?"

"No. I read something Elizabeth had written in a notebook," Jeni answered.

"What did she write?" Her tone was growing defensive.

"She wrote something about telling her mother and her mother figuring out that it was you she had been with."

Danielle sat for a moment in silence. She shook her head, then looked out the window. "Do you have any idea when she wrote it?"

"I'm assuming it was either the night before she was killed or, possibly, the day she was killed." Jeni waited for Danielle to explain, but Danielle sat silently, staring at the carpet. "Were you involved with her?"

"Yes, years ago. We were best friends all through school. When we were in high school, we both realized our feelings. Liz, she had a hard time dealing with it. She fought it real hard, then gave in." She shook her head. "We graduated, and I went on a trip to Europe with a group of kids from school for three weeks. When I got back, Liz told me she couldn't deal with her feelings, that she wanted to go straight. I went away to school, and she married my brother."

"Does Craig know about this?" Jeni asked.

"Yes. He's known since before they were married. He was cool about it. He really loved her. Eventually, Liz realized the feelings were never going to just go away. She felt guilty for what she was putting Craig through and thought he deserved more, so she insisted on the divorce."

Jeni noticed that Danielle had not looked at her since she introduced the subject. Not knowing where to go from that point, she decided to leave and take up the subject with Craig. "Well, again, I apologize for getting so personal. I appreciate your honesty." She stood and awkwardly held the glass of tea toward Danielle. "Tell Robin thanks for the tea."

Danielle took the glass. "Is this going to look bad for Craig?"

"I don't think so." Jeni walked to the door. "Thanks again. I'll be in touch."

Danielle stood inside the doorway and watched Jeni drive away.

"Why is it that this just keeps coming up?" Robin walked into the living room, her face livid with anger.

Danielle turned around, bewildered by Robin's fury. "What are you talking about?"

"I heard everything. You've never gotten over her, have you?" Robin's question received no reply. "Liz has always been a barrier between us. You'd think now that she was dead it would stop, but that just made it worse! All you do is mope around and keep things to yourself." Robin's face grew beet red. "Well, fine. If you want to be alone, I can arrange that!" Robin stormed back towards the bedroom.

"Robin! What the hell's gotten into you?" Danielle followed Robin down the hall.

Robin turned and stabbed at Danielle's chest with her finger. "What's gotten into me? Oh, I don't believe this. I'm not the one who's shut everybody out. I'm not the one who's been hiding my feelings all this time. I'm not the one that holds that damn cat and cries for hours. Face it, Dani, Liz is gone! She's not coming back, and I'll never be her!" She walked forward as she ranted, backing Danielle into the living room.

"Don't you dare talk about Liz! You have no right!" Danielle screamed. "She was my friend. If you can't handle that, then to hell with you!"

"Why can't you just let her go?" Robin's face was filled with rage. She pushed Danielle back onto the couch. "I'm not going to play second fiddle to a fucking ghost!"

Danielle looked away, choking back sobs. "Just leave me alone."

"Oh, that's great!"

A loud knock at the door interrupted their argument. Robin ignored the door and darted down the hall. Danielle, tears now streaming down her face, walked toward the open door. On the other side of the screen door stood Hal Lund and Jim Webber. Danielle brought a hand up to wipe the tears away. "Can I help you?" she said through the screen.

Hal Lund spoke up. "Ms. Harrison, we'd like to talk with you for a minute."

Danielle opened the screen door and stepped out onto the porch. "Yes?"

"We'd like some information about your relationship with your sister-in-law," Jim said.

"Look, this is really a bad time." Danielle's voice was strained with emotion.

"We're sorry to bother you, ma'am, but we've become aware of information that we think you could help us with. We . . ."

"What information?" Danielle asked coldly.

"Ms. Harrison, were you having an affair with your brother's wife?" Jim got directly to the point.

"Do you have a warrant or anything that says I have to talk to you?"

"No, but if we have to, we'll get one," Hal answered.

"I suggest you do that, then. I have nothing more to say." Danielle went back into the house and slammed the door shut.

Hal turned to Jim. "Where the hell were you when God was handing out tact?"

"What are ya sayin'?" Jim asked innocently.

"You don't just blurt out a question like that. You ease into it." Hal stopped as he reached their sedan. He looked back toward the new red Jeep Cherokee that sat in the driveway of Danielle Harrison's home. "Hey, didn't one of the neighbors say they saw a Cherokee poking around Elizabeth Harrison's house the day after she was murdered?"

Jim thought before answering. "Yeah."

"You said you got a description. Does it match Danielle Harrison's?" Hal asked.

"No. If I remember right, it was a big blonde woman. I'll look through my notes." Jim got in the car and began looking through his notebook.

Hal remembered speaking with Danielle. She had said she was in Chicago on business when Elizabeth had been murdered. He made a mental note to check it out.

"Here it is," Jim called out.

Hal got into the driver's seat of the car and shut the door.

"It was the lady who lives in the house just west of the Harrison place. She said a blonde woman, fairly big, parked in the driveway and was walking around the house looking in the windows."

"And she specified that she was driving a Cherokee?"

"Yeah," Jim answered, "a red one."

CHAPTER 23

Jim and Hal had driven in silence for several minutes after leaving Danielle Harrison's home. "So, do you think the sister's involved?" Jim spoke up.

Hal let out a heavy sigh. "I'm not sure of anything at this point." He felt his pockets as he drove.

"What ya lookin' for?" Jim asked.

"What I'd really like is a cigarette, but I'll settle for a stick of gum."

"I told you ya wouldn't make it through today!" Jim grinned.

"Do you see a cigarette between my lips?" Hal turned his gaze away from the road to glare briefly at his partner. "Just give me some gum, would ya?"

Jim found the package of gum on the seat and offered a stick to Hal. "Sounded like Harrison was having a little lovers' quarrel with some woman when we got there, didn't it?"

"Yeah. Something's up. Damn! I wish she would have talked to us." Hal turned into the station's parking garage.

"Think we can get a warrant?" Jim asked.

"No. We don't have enough to go on. We'll have to try for a subpoena, and I don't think we'll get one until Monday." He parked the car and followed his partner into the station.

"Hey! Just the guys I've been looking for," Blake Bartholomew called out as Hal and Jim walked to their desks.

"What's up?" Hal asked as Blake approached his desk.

Blake handed Hal a folder. "Here's the stuff you wanted on RLC. I think you'll find it quite interesting."

"What do you mean?" Hal opened the folder and began looking at the papers it held.

"These, here." Blake pulled two photocopies from the file. "These were the shares in RLC that went to Connor's daughter, Elizabeth Harrison, when he died." He pointed to another photocopy. "This shows that she sold those shares to William Bradford shortly after that."

Hal raised his eyebrows. "That is interesting."

"That's not it, though. We compared the signatures on these with Elizabeth Harrison's signature, and they don't match. These were forged."

"You're positive?" Hal asked.

"Pretty much. Here's the clincher, though. Bradford took out a loan to buy these. At the time, he was up to his neck in financial problems. He shouldn't have been able to get a loan for a loaf of bread. The loan was co-signed by Helen Connor." Blake thumbed through the papers until he found the one he was looking for. "Here's a copy of the loan contract. And," Blake added, "the loan was paid off in full four months after it was taken out. Paid off by a guy who was too broke nine months earlier to keep up on his mortgage payment."

"Have you got Bradford's personal finances?" Hal questioned.

"We're in the process of getting them. Jeffers is still down at the bank going through this stuff. I wanted to get this to you as soon as possible."

"Thanks, Blake." Hal stood and gathered the papers. "Jim, don't get comfortable. We've got a visit to pay to Helen Connor. I think there's more to her relationship with Bradford than just business."

*   *   *

The drive to Helen Connor's home was becoming a familiar route to Hal. He pulled into the driveway and turned to Jim. "We need to handle this carefully."

"You do the talkin', pal. I left my tact in my other suit," Jim said sarcastically.

Hal rang the bell, and he and Jim waited for an answer. After a second ring, Jim began pounding on the door. A few minutes passed, and it was evident that either no one was home, or they were not going to answer the door.

Hal pulled out of the driveway and headed down the street. Jim looked at him questioningly. "What now? Do we go down to RLC?"

Hal slowed to a stop at the corner and watched a black Ford truck drive past. On the door of the truck was a sign that read RLC Construction. "Maybe we won't have to." He watched as the truck pulled into Helen Conor's driveway. He turned around and pulled up behind the truck.

"Gentlemen." Bill Bradford stepped from the truck and greeted Hal and Jim.

"We're looking for Mrs. Connor. Would you know where we can find her?" Hal inquired.

Bill looked over his shoulder at the house. "I don't know where she is." He noticed Hal looking at the soiled flannel jacket he wore over his shirt and tie. He took it off and tossed it onto the seat of the truck. "I've been at one of the sites. You wouldn't believe how filthy your clothes can get just walking through, so I keep some kick-around clothes handy," he explained.

"You wouldn't mind answering a few questions, would you?" Hal asked.

Bill took an uneven step back toward his truck. "If it's questions about Helen's daughter, I don't think I can help you much."

"Actually, we need some information on RLC stock. We understand Elizabeth Harrison sold you some shares a few years back." Hal locked his gaze on Bradford's eyes.

"Look, if you want to talk to me, you'll have to do it through my lawyer." Bill turned and climbed back into the cab of his truck.

Hal noticed the muddy, steel-toed Red Wing boots Bill Bradford was wearing.

Hal stepped forward, grabbing the truck's door before it closed. "Mr. Bradford, what size shoe do you wear?"

CHAPTER 24

The snow fell silently, blanketing the ground with a thick layer of glistening white powder. Jeni stood at her living room window, watching the peaceful storm.

"What was it that finally gave it away?"

Jeni turned to her brother, who sat near the fire.

"Well, the missing button on Bill Bradford's jacket was what really tipped him off. I guess Detective Lund played him right, and the guy confessed later at the station."

"Why did he kill her?" Tom asked.

"He had been having an affair with Elizabeth's mother for years. He was a big gambler and at one point had lost most of his money. Helen Connor, Elizabeth's mother, kind of kept this Bradford guy under her thumb by bailing him out and blackmailing him," Jeni explained. "They got worried that when Elizabeth filed for a divorce she would discover the shares she was supposed to have inherited when her father died, you know, when they went over their finances and assets. But that wasn't the whole thing."

"What?" Tom was engrossed in the story.

"The last straw, so to speak, was when Elizabeth told her mother that she was getting a divorce because she was gay."

"Really?"

"Yeah. Helen was involved in all kinds of civic affairs, and to her, appearances were everything. She would rather die than have news of her daughter's homosexuality go public. Sick, isn't it?"

"Sad is what it is." Tom shook his head.

Jeni took a sip from her mug of coffee. "Anyway, Detective Lund got him to confess, and he said Helen had put him up to it and blackmailed him into doing it. She, of course, denied the whole thing. But then Lund went back over company records and found out that Robert Connor had fired Bradford, who was a foreman at the time, two days before he was killed in an accident. Now they're trying to prove that Helen and Bradford rigged that accident and collected on the insurance money and everything else."

Tom encouraged Jeni to go on with the story. "So, how did he do it?"

"He waited by the doors Elizabeth always left work through. When she passed him on her way out to her car, he pretended to be shopping for his wife. He waited a few minutes after Elizabeth left and walked out to her car. She couldn't get it started, because he had disconnected the ignition wire. He offered to give her a ride and to come back and fix it.

"When he took her home, he asked if he could go in and call his wife to tell her he'd be late. He actually called Helen's number. Then he went out to the garage to supposedly look for some sort of tool while Liz changed her clothes. He called her out there, and when she walked out, he hit her in the back of the head with a tire iron. She fell forward and hit her head on a plywood counter. He hit her again a few times and then wrapped her in a tarp he had laid on the floor, pulled his truck into the garage, and put her in the back." She took another sip of coffee. "Sometime that night, he dropped her car off in Park City and dumped the body up Emigration Canyon. Then they set her husband up to look guilty."

"How did he get the car up to Park City?" Tom asked.

"Well, he told his son he had to go to Park City for a meeting and was riding with someone else, but that they were staying overnight, so he would need a ride back. His son went up and got him."

"That's amazing." Tom shook his head. "Was she really having an affair with the sister-in-law?"

"No. They had been romantically involved in high school, but not after Elizabeth's marriage." Jeni sipped her coffee. "You know, I'm really glad I've gotten to know Danielle. It's helped me realize that she and Robin, her companion, are basically just like any other couple. They have their arguments, they have their hard times, but it's a solid relationship. It doesn't seem so odd to me now."

"So, they really wanted you back at the district attorney's office, huh?" Tom asked.

"Yeah, but I like what I'm doing." Jeni's lips curved upward in a broad smile.

"My little sister. Who would have thought you'd be solving murder cases and defending the lives of innocent men?" Tom elbowed his sister lightly in the ribs. "I'm pretty proud, Jen."

"Thanks, Tom, but I didn't solve it."

Tom smiled at Jeni. "Well, I'm still very impressed."

"You've been here for over an hour, and all we've done is talk about what's going on with me. How are things with you?"

"Great. The traveling is a little hard to get used to. I hate being away from Susan and the kids, but the money I'm getting is worth it."

"Do you like what you're doing now?" Jeni asked.

"Yeah. I can't wait until I can retire, though. The golfing is great in St. George!" Tom looked at his watch. "I'd better get to the airport. My plane leaves at four, and I still have to check in and get a seat assignment." He stood.

Jeni put her coffee on the end table and stood up to hug her older brother. "It's good to see you, Tom."

"It's good to see you, too." He put his coat on and walked toward the door. "Hey, when do we get to meet this guy? I keep hearing wonderful things about him from Mom and Dad."

"Craig and his son, Ryan, are going to Mom's for Thanksgiving dinner with me next week. Will you be there?"

"Yeah, we're coming up." Tom leaned over and kissed Jeni's cheek. "See ya, Jen."

"Bye." Jeni closed the door. She went to the window and watched as her brother drove away. The snow glistened as it fell on the grave markers across the street. As she watched the flakes flutter above the headstones, she was overcome with emotion. A great deal of sadness for all the victims, a little guilt over her own good fortune, and an overwhelming feeling of determination to make a difference.

CHAPTER 25

"Have you got the glasses?" Hal asked Jean as she got out of the car.

"Yes." She pulled the collar of her coat up around her neck tightly. "It's really starting to come down, Hal."

"Bear with me, babe." Hal walked over to the edge of a huge hole, his feet squishing in the mud that mixed with the falling snow. "Come on!" he called to his wife.

"I'm coming." Jean made her way through the muck and snow to join her husband. "You're crazy, you know that?"

"I know I'm crazy about you." He grinned at his wife. "And I'm crazy about our new house."

Jean looked down into the muddy hole where their house would be built. "I'm not quite ready to move in yet, hun."

Hal popped the cork from a bottle of spumante and poured a little of the sparkling wine into the glasses he and Jean were holding. He looked into his wife's shimmering green eyes. "Here's to our future." They toasted each other and sipped from their glasses. "Hurry, finish your glass."

Jean drank the few sips he had poured into her crystal flute.

"Now, throw it down there." Hal motioned to the bottom of the hole the construction company had dug for the foundation of their home.

"These are expensive glasses!"

Hal tossed his glass into the mud. Jean shook her head and laughed, then tossed her glass next to his. Hal looked down at them for a moment, then looked out over the ground that would someday be their lawn. As he noticed the bitterbrush they would have to pull up before laying sod, he felt a twinge of sadness. Hal took a deep breath of the crisp November air and turned to his wife. "Mrs. Lund, would you accompany me to dinner?" He stuck his arm out for Jean to hold onto.

"I'd be honored, Lieutenant."

Look for ANGELA K. BLACK'S
second novel:

DEATH PERCEPTION

Coming Soon!